The Christmas Gift

Emily Walters

The Christmas Gift

Published by Emily Walters

Copyright © 2019 by Emily Walters

ISBN 978-1-07532-273-0

First printing, 2019

www.EmilyWaltersBooks.com

PRINTED IN THE UNITED STATES OF AMERICA

Dedication

I want to dedicate this book to my beloved husband, who makes every day in my life worthwhile. Thank you for believing in me when nobody else does, giving me encouragement when I need it the most, and loving me simply for being myself.

Table of Contents

Chapter 1

"It's not ready," Morgan said. Everyone in the conference room turned around to look at her with

"I don't understand why you can't suck up your dislike for my mother for just this one day!" Jennifer shouted at her husband, Darren. "It's almost Christmas, for crying out loud."

"Why should I? The woman has never had a nice word to say about me. She got drunk at our wedding and made the most inappropriate wedding toast that has ever been uttered. Who tells a roomful of guests that her only hope is that the newlyweds don't procreate before their inevitable divorce?" he shouted back.

"Let it go already, Darren. Like you said, she was drunk and that is ancient history," Jennifer scowled.

"Ancient history? That was only the beginning, Jennifer. The woman insults me anytime I get near her. Why should I ruin a perfectly good holiday by spending it in the company of a woman who loathes me for no good reason? I've never done anything to deserve the treatment I get from her. Nothing at all!" he said, exasperated with the entire conversation. It was the same argument they had every single time something came up that involved her mother.

"Look, I know she isn't a ray of sunshine, but she is my mother and it is Christmas. It has been years since we've been able to spend Christmas together as a family. I go to your family's Christmas gathering every year, but you always refuse to go to mine. Do you know how awkward it is to go by myself time after time and have to make up excuses as to why you can't be there?" she barked.

"Then don't make excuses. Tell them all the truth. Tell them all that I am not there because your mother is a miserable excuse for an in-law. Tell her, in particular, that I'm not there because she doesn't really want me there. She just wants to complain about me not being there. If I actually turned up, she would make a point of attempting to emasculate me at every turn," he stated, feeling more agitated by the moment.

"I don't even know why I argue with you about this. I can't believe you won't do this for me, just once," she said spitefully.

"Well, believe it," he spat back, turning to leave the room.

"We have to get ready to go shopping," she called after him. "It is getting late and I've had an already busy day at work."

"Fine," he yelled back, stomping down the hallway toward the shower before she could get hers.

Jennifer leaned against the counter and exhaled slowly. Things weren't always like this. She could still remember when she had met Darren. It was their junior year of college and they had ended up beside one another in a sociology class. A required social experiment had set them up as partners and they quickly found that they were attracted to one another's quirky sense of humor and style, but neither had tried to be anything more than friends.

Then, after ending up at the same party, things had changed. Darren had asked her out and it was the beginning of everything for them. Darren had been handsome and thoughtful. He was an English major, a geek. His passion for books, theater and most importantly, her, had been overwhelming. She smiled as she thought of all the nights they had spent curled up together on his apartment sofa with him reading to her.

Her thoughts were interrupted as Darren returned from the shower in a towel. She glanced up at him, admiring his bare chest and long legs. Even after all these years, he was still a very attractive man. His deep green eyes and short sandy curls framed his almost delicate face. It was in sharp contrast to his toned, athletic body, which he did little to maintain other than working around their lawn and garden with a bit of hiking tossed in once or twice a month.

"I'm done with the shower," he told her, wandering toward their bedroom to get dressed, presumably.

Jennifer didn't bother to acknowledge him. Once he was gone, she made her way to the shower, taking her time beneath the hot water. She was halfway through rinsing her hair when the water began to grow cool. Anger flooded over her as she finished rinsing off in nearly ice-cold water and stepped out to dry off. Typical that he used all the hot water before her shower. Why was he so inconsiderate?

She could hear the television, so Darren was finished dressing. Heading to the bedroom, she began to get ready, tossing on a pair of yoga pants and an oversize T-shirt with some sneakers. Quickly drying her long dark hair, she pulled it up in a loose bun and settled for a little mascara and lip balm in the way of makeup. She used to take more pride in her appearance, but Darren had never seemed to notice. Of course, he was quick to point it out if he felt she was dressed down, but not so much as a compliment if she made an effort. Why bother?

"Are you ready yet? Is that what you are wearing?" came Darren's voice from the bedroom door.

"What do you mean? There is nothing wrong with this," she said, noting that he was dressed in a pair of khaki pants and a green shirt that only brought out his eyes that much more.

"Not if you are headed to a fast food joint for a burger," he said, rolling his eyes.

"If you have something to say, don't mince words. Just say it, Darren," she told him. Her dark brown eyes were even darker as she glared at him from where she sat at her dressing table.

"Okay, fine. You don't ever dress up anymore. If it doesn't have elastic in the waist or isn't shaped like a tent, you keep it hanging in the closet. You barely wear any makeup and I can't remember the last time that you did more than pull your hair up into a ponytail or bun," he said.

"Well, perhaps if you weren't always rushing me, I might. You took your time in the shower. Thanks for not leaving enough hot water for me, by the way," she said, feeling angry again.

"Who was rushing you? I was sitting in the living room watching television until you were ready," he said.

"Yeah? And why did you come to the bedroom just now? The first thing you asked was if I was ready," she said.

"I had thought that if you were ready, we might have time to go somewhere decent to eat. It's not like you were planning on cooking here. You never cook for me. It's all takeout or frozen and I even have to pick up or fix that for myself. It's always the same every stinking day. What has happened to you?" he said, sounding frustrated.

"My mother was right. You really are a jerk," she shouted at him. "Forget shopping, I don't feel like going right now."

"Of course you don't," he retorted, disappearing from the doorway and down the hall. She heard the jingle of his keys and the sound of his car starting up. No doubt he was headed down to the Salty Dog for a few beers with his buddies. They could all sit around and commiserate about how awful their lives were.

***

"I will have a Guinness," Darren said to the bartender. Looking around the place, he could see other guys his age or older, all sitting around drowning their sorrows in a good beer. It was sad that this was where he felt most comfortable these days. Nodding in thanks as his beer was delivered, he thought about Jennifer. He knew he had been hard on her and he felt ashamed. She was a good woman, a good person.

It just seemed like lately she didn't care about him or herself. He loved her. It was fairly certain that he had loved her since the moment he laid eyes on her and he always would love her, but he couldn't seem to do anything to please her. All his life, he had wanted to write, but that would hardly pay the bills. So, instead, he had settled for the publishing business. It was a hard thing to get into and he had been forced to settle for a junior editor position. It wasn't ideal, but it would open doors to better places. Not only could she not support him in that, she also balked at his suggestion to just start his own publishing company.

"Need another?" the bartender asked.

Darren hadn't realized he had practically gulped down the first beer. He nodded to the bartender, who quickly gathered him another beer and sat it down in front of him.

"Thanks," Darren told him glumly. Here it was almost Christmas and he was sitting in a bar full of miserable men instead of at home enjoying a quiet holiday evening with his wife. How had things gotten so far off course? He wanted desperately to fix things, but had no idea how. Jennifer was the love of his life and yet, he had never felt so far away from a person in his life.

After the second beer, he decided it was time to head home. This place was even more depressing than the way he and his wife seemed to exist together these days. A part of him hoped she would greet him with open arms and tell him everything would be okay, but it wasn't likely. He made his way home to the dark house he knew he would find.

Pulling into the driveway, he noted the darkened windows of the house. It was just as he thought; she had gone to bed without so much as calling to see if he was okay. What if he had drank more than a couple of beers and needed a ride home? He doubted that she would have even answered the phone for him. It broke his heart that things had gotten so bad between them. Letting out a deep sigh, he parked the car in the garage and made his way into the house.

***

Jennifer lay down on the bed and stared at the ceiling. She felt defeated. When had this all happened? They were so in love when they were dating. Neither could get enough of the other. The passion they felt for one another was evident to even those around them. Now, it was if the sight of one another just angered both of them. She could remember when they would spend all night making love and fall asleep in one another's arms. At this point, she couldn't even remember the last time they had been intimate. Had they really fallen so far out of love as this?

The following morning, Jennifer awoke to find she had fallen asleep on the bed in her clothes. Darren was not with her, but he was home. She could hear him snoring from down the hall. No doubt he had elected to sleep on the sofa. It was for the best. In the moods they were in last night, his presence in the bed after being out drinking would have just culminated in yet another argument. It took every ounce of her resolve not to just pull the covers back over her head and stay there, but she finally mustered up enough resolve to get up.

She washed her face and brushed her teeth before changing into a pair of black slacks and a vibrant red shirt. Letting her hair down, she brushed it until it was smooth, applying some hair balm to the ends to add a bit of luster. Finally, she applied her makeup, carefully accenting her features. Her mirror reflected the image of a dark beauty she hadn't seen in a while. Perhaps Darren was right in saying she hadn't cared much for her appearance lately. Perhaps she should stop stripping down into sweats and a ponytail every day after work. Would it make a difference though? Making her way to the living room, she woke him up.

"Darren, we really need to get our Christmas shopping done today. We will both be at work the next two days, so if we don't, we'll won't be able to do it until Christmas Eve," she told him.

"Okay. I'll be ready in a few minutes," he said. Sitting up on the edge of the sofa, he looked her up and down. "You look beautiful. I'm sorry for what I said last night. I was just angry," he told her.

"Yeah, that's fine," she said casually. As apologies went, it was pretty halfhearted. Seemed all they did was apologize to one another these days. It was getting old and had lost much of its meaning.

Jennifer's phone rang from where she had left it on the kitchen counter. She went to answer it, finding that it was her best friend, Marilyn. They began talking about all of the holiday festivities that were coming up and lost track of the time. She had been talking for quite some time when she realized that Darren had already showered, changed and was sitting in the living room waiting for her.

"I have to go, Marilyn. I'll talk to you later," she said. Ending the call, she stuck her phone in her pocket and headed to the living room.

"Oh, finally decided to get off the phone?" Darren asked.

"Don't start," Jennifer replied.

"You are the one complaining that we need to get our Christmas shopping done. I got up, got dressed and have been waiting for over an hour for you to stop yakking on the phone," he replied dryly.

"We would already have gotten it done if you weren't always taking a nap. Sounds like someone sawing logs in here for hours at a time. No one else can sleep or think, but you sure seem happy. I guess that is all that matters," she said.

"Always taking a nap? Do you know how hard I work? I think I'm entitled to a nap when I want one.

I'm surprised you'd even notice with all the noise yours and Marilyn's gabbing creates," he said.

"Oh yeah, you work really hard. Too bad you don't get paid for all that work. You spend long hours doing a job that they don't pay you crap to do. Why? You could do so many other things that would pay better and have fewer hours, but no, you want to work long hours as a junior editor," she groaned.

"I've told you that I won't always be a junior editor. A higher position will open up," he growled.

"When, Darren? WHEN? When we are old and gray and completely broke? I make really good money as a realtor, but it all goes to pay our bills since you don't make much of anything," she hurled back at him.

"It's a good place, Jennifer. I've got my foot in the door and I know where I want to be when things work out for me. They will. You just have to be patient," he told her solemnly.

"Yeah, that is what I keep hearing. Problem is, I'm not seeing it . . . just hearing it," she said, turning to leave the room.

"Perhaps things would be different if you had any faith in me at all. I could be well into the process of getting my own business off the ground by now," he snapped back.

"We don't have the money to sink into a business that may or may not make it, Darren. Be realistic," she said in a frustrated tone.

"Look. Let's just stop this and go get our Christmas shopping done," he said, his voice edgy.

"Forget it. I lost the urge. If people don't get presents, I'll just tell them it is because I'm married to a poor man," she scoffed as she continued walking away.

Darren stood looking at her, feeling completely lost. Why did they do this day after day? His only consolation was that they obviously loved one another or they wouldn't keep doing it, but at what point did all the pettiness overcome what was once a beautiful relationship?

***

Much of the rest of the day and into the night was spent just avoiding one another. Jennifer ate some leftover Chinese food from the fridge while Darren went out to eat. She was grateful for the time without him.

Over the course of the next couple of days, she found herself remembering all of the good times fondly. There had been a time when she and Darren were inseparable. It seemed that these days, they were more apt to do whatever they could to stay away from one another. Before she realized it, their last day of work before the holiday had come and gone. It was Christmas Eve and they still had not done their final shopping.

After the usual arguments, they finally made their way to the local mall. It was crowded with frantic people picking over the remnants left behind by those who had gotten done before the last minute. None of that did anything to improve their temperament and they found themselves bickering over the smallest of things.

"I think we should just get your mother a funnel and a bottle of vodka. It would most likely be her favorite Christmas gift," Darren said snidely.

"Really, Darren? It's Christmas. Can't you lay off my mother even for a few days?" Jennifer replied.

"I doubt it. She certainly never lays off me, so I don't see any reason why I should," he replied. Jennifer stood scowling at him, laying the silk scarf she had been considering buying for her mother back down on the department store display. How could something as simple as selecting a scarf get so ugly, so fast?

"Listen, why don't you go grab something for your parents and I'll go see what I can find for my sister and nephew. I don't think I can stand one more moment of arguing with you about nothing of consequence," Jennifer told him.

"Fine with me," Darren replied, heading in the opposite direction. Jennifer found herself staring after him for a moment. At what point had it become more appealing for him to get far away from her than it was to get closer? She picked the scarf back up and carried it to the counter. Her mother would love it, no matter what Darren thought. A few moments later, she was outside the store and looking in the window of a nearby toy store at the small robotic toys on display.

"Merry Christmas, young lady!!!" boomed a voice from behind her. She turned to find a cheesy-looking store Santa standing behind her. His cap wasn't quite the same color as his coat and neither matched the dingy shade of his pants. The fake beard he was wearing looked like he had glued a bunch of cotton balls together and hung them from his face. He didn't seem like the normal type they had in place at this mall, but here he was.

"You too," she said without conviction.

"Come on. I didn't hear any holiday spirit at all in that. Tell old St. Nick what you'd like for Christmas," he said, still smiling at her. He had red-tinted cheeks and scuffed black boots.

"I'd like a husband who is exactly what I always wanted," she said sarcastically before turning to walk away.

"And what would that sort of husband be like?" he asked, still smiling broadly through his bushy cotton-like beard.

Jennifer paused, turning back toward him and looking him in the eye. Of course it didn't matter, but she began to answer him. Somehow, it seemed to make her feel a little better to indulge herself in the fantasy of what her life could be like with the perfect man for even just a few moments. She smiled whimsically as she began to describe her perfect mate.

"He'd be tall, attractive, passionate, and wealthy. Most of all, he would be considerate and always think of me first. He'd bring me flowers and not expect me to cook and clean up after him all the time. I could take him to my mother's house without having an argument about it. In fact, he would adore my mother and enjoy going," she replied, a faraway look in her eyes as she thought how much better that would be than her endless battles with Darren.

"That is a hefty order, young lady," the Santa said in a jolly tone.

"I don't think so. I think I deserve it. Besides, it is too late for all that. I just wish things could be the way I want them for once. Bye, Santa," she said, turning again to walk away from him. She continued to think about how much better her life could have been with the right man in it.

"Be careful what you wish for," he replied to her disappearing figure. His eyes twinkled a bit as he headed a little further down the line of stores in this section of the mall.

***

Finishing up his shopping in a nearby store a bit later, Darren stepped out to look around for Jennifer. They hadn't made plans to meet back up so he just assumed that he should go back to where they parted ways. He had been waiting there impatiently for over an hour when a store Santa approached him.

"You look like a man that has a Christmas wish," the Santa said, smiling broadly.

"I could use a lot more than one," Darren said.

"I'm afraid that one is all I can give you, son," the man in the Santa suit replied.

"I guess if I only have one, I'd like a new wife. I'd like the wife that I should have had all along. One that looks good and does all the things a good wife should do," he laughed.

"Sounds like you are a bit disappointed in what you have now," Santa replied.

"You don't know the half of it. She just doesn't care. Doesn't take care of herself and doesn't take care of me," he replied in a hurt tone.

"And you want a woman that will wait on you?" Santa said curiously.

"I don't want a doormat that scrubs floors and cooks all day. I want a woman that can stand on her own. I'd like one that doesn't need me to take care of her, but is glad that I am with her. She would be beautiful. You know, like one of those classy model types you see on the cover of women's magazines. Of course, she would also be smart and sweet. She would always be thinking of me and doing things to please me. Just a woman who doesn't have to take care of me, but wants to anyway," he said wistfully.

"What if that meant you would have to give up your current wife?" Santa asked.

"No big deal. I don't think she wants to be with me anyway. It would probably be the best day of her life if she woke up with someone she actually liked," Darren laughed.

"And what about you? Would it be the best day of your life?" Santa asked.

"I don't know, but it would definitely be an improvement over what is going on now!" Darren told him.

"Well, if that is what you want, then that is what you want," Santa replied. "Merry Christmas to you!"

"Right," Darren replied, laughing off the notion that a two-bit store Santa could ever grant him such a wish. Instead, he found his current wife walking toward him. They returned home in silence and climbed into their bed, where they fell fast asleep.

***

Jennifer found herself being awakened hours later as Darren shook her softly, leaning over her.

"Jennifer, Jennifer, are you awake?" he asked.

"Well, I certainly am now," she replied, blinking at him as she focused on his face. He looked quite distraught. She immediately sat up in bed to get a better look at him. "What is wrong?"

"I had the most horrible dream," he replied.

"About what?" she asked, suddenly concerned for him. It was obvious that he was disturbed by whatever it had been.

"I dreamed you were gone," he said quietly.

"What do you mean by 'gone'?" she asked.

"I don't know. I just woke up and you weren't here. I kept looking for you and couldn't find you. It was horrible," he said, reaching for her hand.

"It's okay," she told him, in a soothing voice.

"Yes, it is now," he replied, pulling her closer to him. "I am so sorry for the way I act sometimes. You are my heart and soul."

"It's okay. We both have been pretty heinous to one another lately," she replied.

Darren smiled down at her, pulling her into a passionate kiss. Jennifer let the petty arguments of the day go, her body responding to his in a vaguely familiar ritual. It had been months since they had made love, but their bodies came together in perfect harmony. A familiar ache consumed them, their passion reigniting until they were completely afire.

Falling asleep with her cradled in his arms, Darren felt more at peace than he had in ages, at least for a while. He awoke with a start hours later, startled by a loud crash from downstairs. Jennifer didn't stir from her sleep. Slowly, he crept out of bed and made his way downstairs, grabbing his baseball bat from a corner as he left the room. Shadows fell across the living room as he rounded a corner into the living area and looked around. Nothing seemed amiss.

He jumped as the crashing sound rang out once again through the house. It was coming from outside the front door. Being very cautious, he walked to it and slowly opened it. Just as he did, a gust of wind caught the metal storm door and slammed it against the frame, sending glass flying everywhere as the center window broke into shards.

"Holy crap!" he exclaimed, brushing the glass off his shirt and checking his skin for any cuts.

"What is going on down here?" Jennifer suddenly called out from the top of the stairs.

"You didn't latch the storm door and it was slamming. The glass just broke everywhere," he growled at her.

"Me? Why is it my fault? You could have just as easily left it ajar," she scowled at him, not walking down the stairs.

"You were the last one in the door and I've told you over and over to make sure you shut it just so something like this wouldn't happen," he told her angrily, calming a bit now that he had determined he wasn't cut, but feeling agitated that she hadn't done such a simple thing.

"Well, perhaps if you could have found the time in your ever so busy schedule to fix the latch, I wouldn't have to be worrying whether it closed behind me or not. If you remember, we were both carrying in bags when we came in. I had my hands full too!" she told him.

"Of course, you always find a way to make things my fault, even when you clearly caused the problem," he spat back at her.

"I don't find a way to make them your fault. They are your fault," she replied.

"Look, I don't want to do this. It's late and I'm tired. Just go back to bed. I'll clean this glass up and after

Christmas, I'll go buy a new storm door and just replace the whole thing. I wouldn't want to put you out by asking you to deal with even the most minor hindrance," he said.

"Fine," she replied, turning and storming back up the stairs.

Once she had gone, Darren turned back toward the broken glass, walking carefully across the room toward the kitchen to get the broom. He muttered under his breath as he cleaned up the mess, only growing more agitated by the moment. When he was finished, he discarded the debris, rechecked to make sure what was left of the door was latched so it wouldn't slam anymore and walked to the kitchen, where he poured himself a drink.

It seemed like every day ended this way, no matter how hard he tried to repair things. Was it just a lost cause? He and Jennifer needed some help, some sort of intervention for marriages where someone came in and sorted out what was always setting the both of them off. There was no doubt that he loved her, but something had to change or they just weren't going to make it.

***

Upstairs, in the bedroom, Jennifer tossed and turned. They had ended the day on such a wonderful note she thought and now, here they were, mad at each other again over the simplest little thing. Had she forgotten to close the door? Perhaps she had, but was it really that big a deal? It was just a little broken glass. He hadn't been hurt and the door had needed replacing any way. He seemed to overreact to everything. It was getting very frustrating always arguing with him.

Perhaps they needed marriage counseling, but that just seemed so foreign to her. They loved one another, didn't they? Why weren't they able to just work out their differences without some stranger picking through their brains and refereeing their discussions? So many people she knew went to those sort of things and ended up divorced anyway, convinced that their problems couldn't be surmounted. Losing Darren was the last thing she wanted, but she also didn't want to spend the rest of her life with someone that was always so mad at her for the littlest thing.

She could still hear him downstairs sweeping up glass and complaining out loud. Pulling the pillow over her head, she began crying. It was Christmas and all she could wish for right now was whatever would end this nonsense between them. As the tears subsided, she fell into a restless sleep, tossing and turning as she tried to stave off the bad dream that invaded what little peace she might have felt.

Chapter 2

Darren awoke just as the sun began to stream into the bedroom window. It was Christmas Day and Jennifer would be after him first thing about going to her mother's. The best thing he could do was get up and get moving before she did. Pulling back the covers, he sat up on the edge of the bed and blinked, trying to refocus on the things around him. For a moment, he considered that perhaps he was just dreaming.

Something felt out of place as he rubbed his eyes, wiping the sleep residue from them to take in his surroundings. Where was he? This wasn't his bedroom. Had he somehow been sleepwalking and wound up in a strange place? His heart pounded as he flew up out of the bed and took a look around, ready to dart out the door if he was discovered by whoever lived here.

Wait, he had not been alone. Though he hadn't looked over for Jennifer, he had noted the lump in the bed beside him and felt her slight weight indenting the area of the bed beside him. He turned back to look and gasped, quickly realizing how loud the noise had been. What was going on here?

His gaze roamed across the sleeping figure in the bed. It wasn't Jennifer. Darren panicked. Not only had he wandered into someone else's home, but he had been sleeping next to an unknown woman that was definitely not his usual frumpy wife. He was about to hurry out the door, when she stirred and opened her eyes. He froze as they fell squarely on him and he waited for her to scream, unable to shake free of his paralysis. Instead, she smiled and patted the bed beside her.

"What are you doing out of bed so early, darling? Come back in and snuggle with me a while," she said sweetly, still patting the empty side of the bed he had just vacated with long slender hands that had been perfectly manicured. Her long, pristine red nails made it obvious that whoever this woman was, she did not work hard for a living.

"What?" he managed to get out of his mouth. She seemed to know him. His mind raced to remember the events of last night. He and Jennifer had not been happy with one another and had bickered in the early hours after midnight. She had gone up to their room, while he made himself comfortable with some heavily spiked eggnog on the sofa. One cup had turned into two and that had turned into more than he could really remember. Last thing he remembered was watching "A Christmas Story" on television.

"What's wrong, Darren? You look positively bewildered. Are you okay?" she asked, sitting up in the bed.

He barely noticed the look of concern on her face as the duvet fell away to reveal a very skimpy satin teddy hugging what could only be described as the perfect body. She was thin, but possessed curves in exactly all the right places. Her skin looked smooth, too smooth. In fact, she reminded him of one of the porcelain dolls his mother had in her curio cabinet, remnants from her childhood. Now, looking at her, he registered the notion that she was exactly the sort of woman he had described last night to that store Santa that granted him a Christmas wish. An eerie feeling passed over him. There was no way. It simply wasn't possible.

"I'm fine. I think," he replied, feeling incredibly confused. Spotting what appeared to be a bathroom on the opposite side of the room, he excused himself and went in, shutting the door quickly behind him and looking in the mirror. It was his face, alright. So, he was still him, but where was Jennifer and who was the woman in the bed? Had he somehow gotten drunk last night and snuck out to spend the night with another woman? The thought that he might have cheated on Jennifer horrified him. Despite their problems, that just wasn't him.

"Darren, are you sure you are okay?" the woman called to him from outside the door.

"Um, yes. Yes, I'm fine," he called back, not feeling fine at all. Maybe this was just a dream. He turned on the water, splashing it on his face and smacking one hand against his cheek to see if he felt it. It stung. Perhaps it just stung in the dream. Opening the medicine cabinet, he pulled out a bottle of antibiotics. The side of the bottle read "Darren Johnson." They were his, though for what, he wasn't sure. Beside it was a container of birth control pills. At least if he had done something stupid, it was hopefully somewhat safe. The name on the bottle read "Barbara Johnson." The round plastic container clattered loudly as he dropped it in the sink, even more bewildered.

"Honey, I'm going to go make breakfast while you shower. Just come down when you're finished," the woman, who he now assumed was Barbara and perhaps his wife in some weird dimension he had landed in, called out to him.

"Okay," he told her, feeling incredibly nauseous. Sitting down on the edge of the large garden tub, he buried his face in his hands and contemplated what was happening here. It didn't seem to be a dream and yet, how could it be real? There seemed to be no doubt that it was real, though.

After a while, he got undressed and turned on the shower, stepping under the water before it had even warmed in hopes that the cold tap would bring him back to reality. When nothing changed, he resigned himself to going downstairs to this strange woman and just letting the day play out. Perhaps the answers would come to him as the day unfolded.

"Are you going to work today?" the woman asked.

"Yes, I guess so," he said, suddenly unsure of anything.

"Okay. I had Belinda clean your study so that you could get right to it. She was given specific instructions not to touch anything on your desk, so she probably didn't dust it. I will do that later so that I can make sure everything goes right back where you like it," she told him.

"My study? I work in there?" he asked, not following what she was saying.

"Of course you do. Where else would you work? Are you feeling okay?" she asked.

"Yeah, I mean, I think so. Listen, I don't think I can eat right now. I'm going to get an early start," he told her.

"No breakfast? That's not like you at all," she replied. "Would you like me to bring you something in a bit after you settle in? I know you don't focus as well on submissions when you haven't had a healthy meal."

"Submissions?" he repeated. When had he started working on submissions from home? Though the publishing house didn't mind if work was taken home for a bit of overnight reading, Jennifer had been strictly opposed. On the occasions he had brought work home with him, it had stayed in his briefcase and he only reviewed it after she was in bed for the night. It often resulted in his being overly tired the next day, but it hadn't been worth the fallout he would get if he was reading rather than tending to whatever she felt he should be around the house.

"Books? It's a bit hard to run a publishing house if you don't take the time to read any of the submissions people sent in, honey. Are you sure you are okay?" she asked thoughtfully.

"Yes. I'm sorry. I just have some things on my mind this morning," he told her. He stepped away from the counter and headed toward one of the side doors.

"I thought you were going to the study?" she said curiously.

"I am," he replied, feeling completely disoriented and anxious.

"Are you taking the long way around?" she laughed, her beautiful head cocked to one side.

"Oh, right. I wasn't thinking," he replied, crossing the kitchen and exiting the opposite door. Hopefully, she would stay in the kitchen and not see him trying different doors until the figured out where it was he was supposed to be going and what he was supposed to be doing there.

***

Nearby, Jennifer was finding herself being shaken awake from a deep sleep. Rolling over, she expected to find Darren standing by the bed with a sour look on his face, as usual. Instead, she found herself looking into the nearly perfect face of a handsome stranger. She screamed and pulled the covers around her.

"Jen? What's wrong?" he asked, a look of shock on his face.

"Who are you? Why are you in my house?" she said, jumping up from the bed. No sooner had the words left her mouth than she began to look around the room. This wasn't her house. Where was she and how did she get here? Her heart thudded loudly against her chest cavity. Her nerves jangled throughout her limbs and tried to escape from the tips of her fingers and toes.

"Last time I checked, I was your husband," he laughed, looking confused.

"Husband?" she repeated slowly, her heart pounding out of her chest.

"Yes. You know, we had that thing with all the people and the formal wear. There was a minister, rings, cake!" he said with a slow laugh.

"I . . ." she began to say, her voice trailing off as she attempted to process what was happening.

"You . . . need to get ready to go to your mom's house. You know how she gets when we are late. Feisty woman, she is. She really cracks me up," he said.

"You like my mother?" she said with a furrowed brow.

"What? Of course I like your mother. Where did that come from?" he asked.

Jennifer looked him up and down for a moment. He was beautiful. Perfect teeth, tanned, dark wavy hair, tall, toned and seemingly with a pleasant disposition where her mother was concerned. The words rattled around in her head as she remembered the Santa from last night. No way. Could something like this really be happening? Yet, here this man was claiming to be her husband and Darren was nowhere in sight.

"I don't know. I'll get ready," she said, looking around at the room they were in. It was huge. Easily four times the size of the one she and Darren shared. Walking slowly over to what she presumed was the closet, she found herself flooded with light by merely opening the door. Inside was a huge walk-in closet with everything perfectly pressed and hanging on either side. At the end was a large revolving shoe rack filled with the most gorgeous shoes. If this was a dream, she wasn't sure that she wanted to wake up. She took her time running her hands across the colorful designer shoes and across the delicate materials of the clothes hanging adjacent to them.

"I'll be downstairs whenever you are ready," he called to her. She heard his footsteps as he made his way to the lower level and began to get ready. Somehow, she knew he wouldn't be back to rush her. She found herself wondering what had become of Darren in all of this as she struggled to comprehend what was happening. Was he okay? She had to hope so. It weighed heavy on her mind as she picked out clothes, showered and dressed.

"There is the love of my life," the man said as she approached him.

"Yes, here I am, here," she replied, wondering to herself exactly where "here" was.

"Are you okay this morning, Jen? You seem like you have something on your mind. Do you need to talk about it?" he asked. She could see the genuine concern on his face, but there was certainly no way she could tell him the truth. For a moment, she envisioned herself telling him that yesterday she had a different husband, but that this morning she had woken up with him. No doubt that would go over quite well.

"I'm fine. I guess I am just thinking about going to mom's. It can be such an ordeal," she replied.

"Ordeal? Since when? Granted, your mother is a bit unorthodox, but you know I find her amusing and she loves me. Don't forget that!" he laughed.

Jennifer was having a really hard time thinking anyone else could love her mother, but perhaps things were very different about her in this bizarre world in which she had landed. If she had a different husband, then what else was different?

"I'm sorry. I don't know what is wrong with me this morning," she replied sheepishly.

"Probably just tired from the holiday rush. I am so sorry that you had to do most of the shopping by yourself. Sometimes work can get really out of hand this time of year. I promise I will make it up to you on our anniversary," he told her with a wink.

Jennifer hoped she didn't look as startled as she felt. The thought of an anniversary with this man wasn't something she was prepared to deal with. It was bad enough that she didn't know where Darren was, but now she had to consider that she was married to the man in front of her. Glancing down at the ring on her finger, she realized it was no longer the simple gold band with a light scroll she and Darren had selected together. Instead, she found herself looking at an ornate gold band and matching engagement ring that must have cost a small fortune.

"It's okay," she said slowly, trying to shake the feeling of doom that seemed to have taken hold of her. It hit her that maybe this was just a dream and she would wake up in the morning to have a good laugh about the whole thing.

"Let's get to your mom's. It's Christmas Day! Aren't you excited?" he asked.

"Yes. Yes, I am," she replied, trying to sound happy. This was either an incredibly vivid dream or she was losing her mind. Reaching for a purse that she didn't remember, like the rest of the things she could see around her, she followed a man whose name she didn't even know out of their house.

"That's my girl," he smiled, kissing her on the cheek as he waited and held the door open for her to exit.

Jennifer looked back at the house they had exited as they approached the car in a large circular drive. It was a mansion by her standards. The large white columns accented the plantation style home surrounded by perfectly groomed shrubs and a manicured lawn. It sat in a row of similar homes divided only by small fences and strips of yard. It was obviously an exclusive neighborhood, but it lacked any imagination whatsoever.

She reflected on the small ranch style home she and Darren shared, with its overstuffed furniture and eclectic decorations. It was cozy and felt like a home should. The one she had just stepped out of felt cold and foreign to her. It was all sharp angles and modern design, like a model living space created for the cover of some interior design magazine. There was no way a house like that could possibly feel like a home for her. Then again, there was no way any house without Darren could feel like a home.

As they traveled across town toward her mother's, they passed through the street where she and Darren lived, but she quickly saw that it looked completely different. Instead of the mixed model homes that used to be on this street, there were now perfect rows of townhouses and condos. Apparently, not only was there no Jennifer and Darren in this world, there was also nothing that had ever been familiar to the two of them. Everything had changed. Jennifer found herself wondering, once again, if maybe this wasn't just a strange illusion.

As the day continued, she slowly began to realize it wasn't a dream. Somehow, she had ended up in another life, with another husband. It didn't make any sense, but there was no other explanation. That Santa had somehow taken what she had told him while angry and made it happen. What was she going to do? Perhaps she had asked for this, but it was never intended to really happen. Now that it had, what was she going to do?

***

As the day progressed, Darren spent a quiet Christmas morning with the woman who he now knew was, by some magic, his wife. He couldn't help but feel overwhelmed by the way she doted on him and cared for him. Not only was she a magnificent creature to look at, but she was so attentive and well groomed. There was not so much as a hint of the slovenly behavior of Jennifer to be found in her. Though he was hesitant to take her to his family's Christmas gathering, she ignored his excuses not to go and insisted that he was being silly. Soon, they were off to his mother's house, arriving to being welcomed with open arms as if nothing was amiss.

"Darren has been positively odd all morning," Barbara laughed. She ran her hand thoughtfully across his shoulders as she spoke. It seemed as foreign as he currently felt.

"My Darren does have his moments, but he is a good boy," his mother said, shooting him a sideways glance with a smile.

"I'm not twelve, Mom," Darren laughed.

"Aw, I think you are embarrassing our guy, Mom," Barbara added.

Darren chuckled at their playful ribbing as he left the room to watch some tube with his dad. Everything still felt strange and surreal, but at least he felt a tiny bit more relaxed. That quickly changed as it came time to open presents. Barbara handed him a silver foiled box with a blue satin bow. He smiled faintly and looked at her apologetically.

"I didn't have time to shop. I didn't get you a present . . . yet," he told her, his eyes downcast.

"It's okay. I know you have been busy," she said, the smile never leaving her face. How could any woman be so understanding? "Go ahead, open yours."

Darren looked at her beaming face, guiltily opening his present. "It's gorgeous!" He momentarily forgot his embarrassment at having not gotten anything for her as his hands ran across the smooth leather covering the journal.

"I remember you looking at it in the shop. I knew you wanted it, but you are always frugal," she laughed.

"I don't know what to say . . ." he began, feeling horrible. He considered all the years he had put so much thought into gifts for Jennifer and now she wasn't here and he was apparently with a woman who he deserved no more than the one he had given up.

"Perhaps you should stop teasing poor Barbara and give her the gift you got her, Darren," his mother said from a nearby chair.

"Mom, I didn't . . . " he began to say, but stopped mid-sentence as his father reached beneath the tree and pulled out a small box, handing it to Barbara before continuing to pass out gifts to others. Darren watched intently as she opened it, pulling from it a very expensive-looking pair of pearl earrings.

"Oh, Darren! They're gorgeous! Put them on me!" Barbara squealed. "I can't believe you bought them for me. Thank you. Thank you so much!"

"You're welcome," Darren replied, wondering how long he had been with this woman. He had obviously been with her somehow in this parallel universe even while he was with Jennifer. At least he felt better that he hadn't neglected to get her a gift. He was obviously making a lot more money now if he could afford a set of pearl earrings like that, the house they lived in and the cars they drove. Still, his mind drifted back to Jennifer. Where was she? That was his main question.

***

Across town, Jennifer slowly began to realize that not only was her new husband great-looking, he was also rich. They took a Jaguar to her mother's house and were having a fantastic day, something Darren would never have done with her.

"Bill, would you like a drink?" Jennifer's mother asked. Jennifer bristled a bit. This always got a snide remark from Darren, but who could really blame him. It was only nine in the morning.

"Maybe later, Mom. I am far more interested in brewing up some of your favorite coffee. I brought you a fresh container from the market," he told her.

"That is so sweet! Coffee does sound nice!" she laughed, putting away the bottle of vodka that she usually had with her morning juice and walking over to help him with the coffee maker. Jennifer was awestruck as he flashed her a knowing smile and winked. She gave him a subtle nod of approval and smiled despite her astonishment.

"Jennifer, I swear. If you would just clone Bill and sell him on dating sites, you would be a millionaire," her mother laughed. Jennifer flushed with embarrassment. Her mother always said the most awkward things.

"I don't think the world is ready for more than one of me, Mom," he joked, while pouring her a cup of coffee and lacing it with just the amount of cream and sugar she preferred. Once he was done, he poured himself and Jennifer each a cup. Jennifer noted that hers was also prepared exactly as she liked it. It made her wonder exactly how long she had been here with Bill. There was obviously more history between them than just waking up together this morning. Had they always been together in some alternate dimension? Everything about this was just unbelievable.

Jennifer and her new spouse spent most of the morning in the kitchen drinking coffee and nibbling at food as they prepared for guests to arrive at noon. Usually, her mother was well inebriated by then, but today was very different. She was just as sober and fresh-faced as she had been when they arrived and Bill seemed to be focused on keeping her that way, offering her non-alcoholic drinks so subtly that it wasn't even obvious to Jennifer what he was doing at first.

Of course, there was only so long that could last. By the time afternoon desserts had been gathered, her mother had finally moved away from Bill's sobriety program and found a nice bottle of wine to go with her slice of Aunt Bettie's homemade cherry pie. Before evening rolled out, she was rapidly approaching her usual caustic self.

"Come on, Jennifer. Let's clean some of this up and get home," Bill coaxed, pulling her away from the still gathered relatives laughing raucously in the living room.

"You don't have to help clean up," she told him as they walked toward the kitchen.

"What? Of course I do. Let's get some of this cleared out and get home to open our own gifts," he told her.

Jennifer looked at him, trying to seem excited. Two things were suddenly on her mind. The first was what sort of present could a complete stranger get her that she would like? It had always been her biggest thing with gifts that they not be so much about the expense as that they be thoughtful. While she and Darren had had their issues, he had always been very intuitive when it came to what gifts would make her happy. The second thing that sprang to mind was wondering if she had gotten him anything and, if she had, it best be under the Christmas tree because she would have no idea where it might be hidden otherwise.

Jennifer was relieved when they finally arrived home and she found that their gifts were neatly stacked under the tree. Bill beamed as he handed her an intricately wrapped box. She accepted it hesitantly, trying to smile at him as if everything about this day was perfectly normal. Opening the box, she found herself looking at a set of car keys. Her eyes were wide as she looked up at him.

"Come on!" he said happily. "Let's go take a look!"

Bill and Jennifer walked out to the garage and pulled the cover from a car she had assumed to be his. Instead, there was a sleek, metallic gray BMW convertible.

"Oh, Bill! I can't believe you bought me a new car! I don't know what to say," Jennifer exclaimed.

"Well, I remember you looking at one parked in front of the library last month when we went to their opening," he replied.

"I don't know what to say. It's beautiful. Thank you," Jennifer replied.

"Anything for the love of my life. Let's take this baby for a ride!" he said, already walking around to get in the passenger side of the car.

Jennifer hesitated for a moment and then hopped in driver's seat and cranked the car. A few moments later, they were roaring down the highway with the top down in the middle of winter. Returning to the house, they were both freezing and laughed as they piled up in blankets in front of the fire to thaw. As Bill attempted to snuggle closer to Jennifer, she realized that though he was now her husband, he was still very much a stranger to her.

"I'm warmer now. Why don't we finish opening our gifts?" Jennifer asked, already on her feet and headed toward the tree. She was surprised to find that there was a gift for him under there and wondered when she had purchased it. Nothing about this world made sense to her. She watched as he opened it and positively glowed, pulling from the box a very nice Omega Prestige wristwatch and marveling over it. It wasn't quite as expensive as the new car she had gotten, but still a very tasteful gift that he had apparently wanted if his reaction to it was any indication.

Later, as the couple prepared for bed, Jennifer located a heavy pair of flannel pajamas and snuggled into her side of the bed. She lay there in the darkness and contemplated the events of the day. This new man never left her side the whole day, even while mingling with her mother's friends and other family members. Even stranger, they all seemed to know him. Not one seemed put off by the fact that her husband was now someone completely different than yesterday. She now also knew that he was named Bill Jenner, according to the way he was addressed by some of the guests at her mother's party, but still she wondered what had happened to Darren.

***

As the day had progressed, both Jennifer and Darren had somewhat accepted that they were now with new spouses. Through some strange miracle, their Christmas wishes had come true. It would seem each had gotten exactly what they asked for, but there was this nagging feeling that something was not quite right. Why could they still remember their old life and where was their original spouse?

Chapter 3

"Mom, do you find anything odd about Bill?" Jennifer asked in a quiet moment alone with her mother the following day when she and Bill returned to help with final cleanup from the party.

"Odd? What do you mean? He seemed the same as he always has. Oh, hon, you two aren't having problems, are you?" she asked.

"No. I don't think so," she said scowling a little. "I just keep wondering what happened with Darren?"

"Darren? Who is Darren?" her mother asked.

"Um, Darren? The husband I had before? He was there when I went to bed and then, yesterday morning, I woke up with a new husband," Jennifer said, hoping her mother could make some sense of this.

"Jennifer, how much wine have you had? Or are you just trying to get one over on your old mom? I may be getting on up there in years, but I only remember one wedding and that was to Bill," her mother said with a laugh.

"I wasn't married before?" Jennifer asked earnestly.

"Of course not. You've been married to Bill since you graduated college. You met him at a charity auction and you've been inseparable ever since. First husband! That's rich! Now, quit giving me a hard time with such nonsense and help me clear these dishes," her mom laughed, shaking her head.

"Yeah. I'm just messing with you, Mom," Jennifer laughed. "Just a Christmas prank of sorts."

"Playing pranks on your mom?" Bill asked as he stepped through the doorway with a load of dishes and began stacking them on the counter by the sink. "You ladies need a good dishwasher?"

"I thought you'd never ask," her mom replied, making room for him at the sink while Jennifer wandered out to clear away some more dishes for them to wash.

There was no doubt that her new husband was the perfect man she had always wanted, but she couldn't help still wonder what had become of Darren. Where was he and how was she going to explain all of this to him? As much as yesterday had been a perfect Christmas, she couldn't help but think about how she had missed Christmas with Darren. Even if things went back to normal tomorrow, they would never get this Christmas together back.

***

After the visit to his mother's, Darren and Barbara had returned home from his family's festivities and begun their own holiday party with some friends and neighbors. Darren still couldn't believe how different things were for him now. His wife was absolutely gorgeous. It turned out that she was a former model, a career that left her with plenty of money. Their house was considerably nicer than the small home he and Jennifer had lived in together. Having previously located the study where he worked, he wandered in, indulging himself in some quiet reflection.

The chatter from their friends drifted into the room through the partially opened door. Though he had come to realize this new life was really happening somehow, he still felt like a bit of a stranger sneaking around someone else's house, rifling through their things. It was going to take some time to get used to it. The thought made him realize that getting used to this meant giving up his former life with Jennifer. The party was great and all, but it was so noisy and busy. He found himself missing the quiet of the home he shared with his former wife. It followed naturally that he felt a loss. He had to admit that, as imperfect as their life was together, he did miss the companionable silence they often shared.

"Darren? What are you doing in here?" Barbara asked as she stepped through the open door with two glasses of wine, handing him one with a smile.

"I'm sorry. I just needed a moment," he replied.

"I know you aren't in here working! It's Christmas! Come on back out to the party," she coaxed.

"I wasn't working. I'll be right there," he told her, smiling softly as he sipped from the glass of wine she had given him.

"I'll be waiting," she told him seductively. Darren was surprised to find that, despite her incredible body and full, pouty lips, he didn't feel as drawn to her as he had thought he would with such a woman. Sure, she was an almost angelic creature, but she wasn't Jennifer. He found himself wondering why he would be granted this wish, but retain the memories of the woman he once loved, still loved, in fact. After a few moments, he returned to the party and tried to mingle with their friends as if he belonged, though he didn't recognize a single face.

Chapter 4

"Let's go, baby!" Barbara said excitedly, already halfway out the front door.

"I'm on my way," Darren replied, grabbing the keys from a bowl on a nearby table. They were headed out to some after-Christmas sales that she wanted to go to. Shopping really wasn't his thing, but he found himself missing a few items he had possessed in his past life and wanted to look for them while she did her thing.

Just as he was about to get into the car, his breath caught in his throat. Across the shrubs between their house and the neighbor's he spotted Jennifer, her hand raised in greeting toward Barbara, who had done the same. She had begun to slip into the passenger seat of a car parked in a large circular driveway outside her home when she spotted Darren exiting the house next door and making his way to his own car. For a moment, their eyes met and they stared at one another.

"Jennifer, we're going to be late," the man on the opposite side of the car said, climbing in behind the wheel of the vehicle. She turned toward him, breaking her eye contact with Darren and closing the door. Though Darren couldn't see her through the tinted windows, he felt certain that she was still watching him as he watched the car back out of their drive.

"Who was that?" he asked Barbara, who stood waiting by the car for him to open the door.

"You are just positively ditsy lately, Darren. I think you are working way too hard, baby. You know them. Bill and Jennifer Jenner, our neighbors next door," Barbara replied.

Everything felt gray for a moment, as Darren realized that he wasn't the only one who had been granted a Christmas wish. Jennifer had gotten one, as well. Though he had to acknowledge that he had wronged her in exactly the same way, he hurt deeply to know that she had wished for someone so completely different than him, someone better. Pangs of guilt and sadness filled him as he climbed into the car to leave for their shopping expedition.

Though Barbara chattered lightly on their way, he couldn't tell you a word she said. His thoughts were racing with how this had all happened and how he was going to live with Jennifer next door to him with another man while he was with another woman. Still, if that is what she had wanted and she got it, who was he to interfere? As much as it pained him, he would let her go. It was only right that she have the husband she deserved rather than a schmuck like him. He would just try to make the best of his new life.

***

In the other car, Jennifer felt devastated. She and Bill had just returned from her mother's house and were going right back out to meet friends for a late lunch. Bill was telling her that they really should do something with their neighbors sometime.

"Who?" she asked, not really comprehending what he was saying.

"Our neighbors, Darren and Barbara. We don't do as much with them as we used to and we should. They are really great people," he said.

"Yeah. Okay. I don't know," she replied idly. Nothing sounded more horrifying to her at the moment.

"Are you okay, Jennifer? You have been odd since yesterday. Is something wrong?" he asked, obviously concerned.

"Oh, uh, no. I'm fine. Just the holiday rush and all. I guess I'm a little tired," she replied.

"That's not like you at all. I hope you aren't coming down with something," he said.

Jennifer smiled weakly at him. If only this were just some sort of fevered hallucination. At least that would make sense. Now, not only was she in some inexplicable new life with a new husband, she was living beside her old husband and his bimbo of a wife.

It was hard to believe that he would rather have some little trophy dish than someone like her, with some intelligence and that truly had loved him. Though she wanted to be mad about it, she just felt like someone kicked her in the stomach. This whole thing was truly unbelievable. Oh well, if that is what he wanted, then let him have it. The last thing she would do was interfere.

***

As days passed everything reminded Darren of Jennifer. Everywhere he went, everything he saw, even his new wife. The differences between Jennifer and Barbara only made him miss Jennifer's quirky ways even more. Barbara was meticulous about everything. The house was spotless, everything was neatly folded and put away, and it always smelled of the most delicious food. She had none of Jennifer's haphazard ways about her. He found himself missing them.

"Honey, would you like me to bring you a glass of water or something to drink?" Barbara called from the kitchen.

"No, I'm fine. I am just reading through some manuscripts," he said.

"You should take a break and enjoy the gorgeous day outside," she told him.

"I know, but I really need to get this done," he told her. The truth was that he had hardly read even a single page of it. His thoughts were all on Jennifer and how much he missed her. There was no other woman that could take her place, not even one handed to him by some Santa who he had given a rundown of what he had thought would be better than the wife he loved dearly.

Before he knew it, bedtime was there and he tucked in early, feigning sleep when Barbara came to bed. She had attempted to achieve some intimacy between them since he had arrived in this place and he had been constantly avoiding it.

"Darren, are you asleep, honey?" she cooed at him.

He let out a little snore for effect. It seemed to do the trick, as she let out a sigh and climbed into her side of the bed, rolling her body to face away from him to sleep. He felt bad that he had to be this way to a woman that obviously loved him and had no clue why her husband had no desire to touch her, but no matter what had happened, he couldn't be unfaithful to Jennifer. A chill went through him as he realized that she might not even remember him and might not be holding back with her own spouse. He tossed and turned the rest of the night, thinking about it.

***

Jennifer watched from where she was working in a flowerbed as Darren emerged from his house in running gear and began jogging down the sidewalk away from her house. Apparently, his new life agreed with him. He had been very much a couch potato while married to her. Though he was never in bad shape, it was just something that had come naturally for him and was not a result of having any type of exercise take place. She could only surmise that he was more interested in his appearance with his current wife. A twinge of jealousy jolted through her as she imagined them together. Quickly shaking it off, she went into the house for her purse and keys, then exited the front door and drove the opposite direction in her new car.

A little further down the block, in the opposite direction, Darren congratulated himself on managing to get out of the house without running into Jennifer. He had stopped to tie his shoe when he had seen her exiting the house and watched from a nearby row of shrubs. She had looked positively radiant as she had left. He found himself missing her even more, but knew that this was what she wanted. Who was he to take away a life that he had never given her? If Bill was what she truly wanted then he would let her have that, but he knew that he would go to his grave loving only her.

***

Both Darren and Jennifer spent quite a bit of time over the next days wondering how much the other knew. It hurt to think that all the great memories that they had shared could have just disappeared so quickly. The only logical explanation for them not to be talking was that the other one was content with their new life. So, as the weeks continued, each felt that their only option was to steer clear of the other and avoid the pain of seeing them with another.

In the instances where it was unavoidable for them to see one another outside their homes, they made every effort to pretend they didn't notice each other and hurried away as quickly as possible to their car or back in the house. Each stuck to their decision not to disrupt the other's perfect new life and just make the best of what they had wished upon themselves. Besides, was their old life so great anyway? There was a reason they both wished for something else.

***

"You did what?" Darren barked at Barbara as she told him her news a few weeks later. Things had been going well between them on a lot of levels. She was even more perfect than just her looks. The house was always immaculate and she cooked for him every day. Though they had staff that could do many of the things she took upon herself, she said she just enjoyed doing it for him. She never hung around the house in her pajamas or an old robe. Every morning, she rose early and showered, dressed to kill and did her hair and makeup so that he never woke up to a frumpy wife.

The one place things weren't perfect was in the bedroom. As hard as he tried, he just had not been able to bring himself to be intimate with her. In his heart and in his head, he was still married to Jennifer and though it was apparent he had slept with this woman prior to when he became aware of his presence here, he couldn't do it now that he knew Jennifer was right next door. Of course, being the perfect wife that she was, she never complained about it and just tried to be understanding of whatever it was he was going through. She was such a wonderful, beautiful woman that he wanted to love her, but he found he just couldn't.

"I invited Bill and Jennifer over for a barbecue," she had said.

"Jennifer agreed to come?" he asked.

"You know, it is funny you should ask that. She didn't really seem very keen on the idea. I don't know if we've offended her somehow or if she has something else on her mind, but I really feel like she was going to say no before Bill jumped in and agreed to come," she said, puzzling over the behavior.

"I see," Darren said. Of course she didn't want to come. The last person she wanted to be around was her old, imperfect husband. She probably couldn't tear herself away from the human Ken doll she was married to now. The thought was immediately followed by his wondering if that were really the case. Did she know? Is that why she was reluctant? Or was it just his imagination that she might be aware of the situation as much as he?

By the time the day of the barbecue arrived, Darren felt like a caged animal. He wanted so badly to say something to her, to see what she remembered, if anything. What if she was just as aware as he was? What if she missed him too? Still, he couldn't say anything. There was a chance that she didn't and that she was happy. He wanted that happiness for her, even if it wasn't with him. He had been a terrible husband and this was his punishment. How could he have known that things weren't much better on the other side of the fence?

***

"I don't know why you want to go over there," Jennifer said to Bill as they got ready to go next door for the barbecue.

"What do you mean? I thought you liked Darren and Barbara? We used to go over there all the time and then everyone just got busy, but I didn't think you had a problem with them. Do you?" he asked, puzzled by her hesitation.

"No, of course not. I just am not up for a barbecue, really," she lied. Bill was an incredible man. She hated lying to him, but the truth would only get her put away for being crazy, in all likelihood. All she could do was just steer clear of Darren as much as possible. She smiled weakly at her new husband and headed out the door he was holding open for her.

***

"Hey, Jennifer! It's so nice to see you again. It's been way too long since we got together," Barbara said brightly as she came to the door. Jennifer tried to smile, but found she had a hard time feigning any friendliness to this woman who was now married to her former husband. Darren was nowhere to be seen as Barbara continued on with her giddy greeting, redirecting her attention toward Bill.

"Where is Darren?" he asked from behind her. "He is not leaving me alone with two beautiful women, is he?"

"Bill, you are always so funny. He'll be with us shortly. I left him in the study on the phone . . . business. He has worked so hard to get it off the ground. I'm so very proud of him," she said. "Come on out to the patio. I've already got everything set up out there."

"Oh, yeah. I heard that he had started his own publishing house. That's fantastic! I always admire people who know what they want and go after it," Bill said enthusiastically.

"Yes, that is incredible for him," Jennifer added, trying not to sound as bitter as she felt. The idea that he could wish her away and just start over with this new woman, getting everything he wanted, was hurtful. More than that, she felt a sense of guilt at the fact that she had not supported him in his efforts to succeed. Perhaps if she had been a better wife they would not be here now. Her thoughts were interrupted as Barbara began to speak again.

"Make yourselves at home. I will go see what is keeping Darren," she told them. Jennifer watched as her perfect form practically glided down the hallway and out of sight.

Looking around, Jennifer could see what impeccable taste Barbara possessed. Their home was gorgeous, decorated in modern, sophisticated tones. She couldn't recall ever having been here before, though conversations leading up to this get-together made it obvious she had. Why could she remember Darren, but not this life? She wondered once if he remembered her. The glance they had shared the first day she had seen him in this new life had made her think he did, but he had done nothing to let her know he was aware since then.

Jennifer still had to consider that he did know and merely chose to stay here with his new wife. It seemed like everything he had ever wanted was embodied in this perfect-looking woman. Even the fact that he apparently had his own business going now made it evident that he was getting what he always wanted and had not been able to accomplish while married to her. She definitely should just let it all go and get on with her own life. Then again, there was such a huge part of her that missed him.

"Darren, what are you doing? Our guests are here," Barbara asked.

Darren looked up from where he sat alone in his study pretending to work, delaying the inevitable. He was going to have to go out there. Letting out a huge sigh, he finally stepped out from behind his desk and left the study with Barbara, making their way to the patio. Seeing Jennifer, it was immediately awkward. She looked fantastic. He was so used to seeing her running around in a ponytail and sweats. Although she wasn't wearing formal attire, it was just a backyard barbecue, she looked well put together today. She hadn't taken as much pride in her appearance in years during their marriage. It would seem the new husband inspired her to maintain her appearance more than he ever had.

"Darren, good to see you again," Bill said, grabbing his hand and shaking it.

"You too," Darren replied, barely able to muster an appearance of friendly banter. Jennifer stood nearby with her back to him, talking to Barbara. He tried not to look at her, instead busying himself with getting the grill going. He took his time, stalling until the women went into the kitchen to get some other things, going in order to avoid conversation.

"So, how is the new business venture going?" Bill asked, standing to one side of the grill with a drink in his hand.

"It's going good. Getting a lot of good responses from people on it. I should be in full swing within about six months," Darren told him, having now had a chance to look through the business stuff over the past weeks.

"That's great. I'm really glad to hear it. You know, when you slow down, we should get together more. Toss back a few drinks down at the clubhouse together," Bill replied.

"Clubhouse? Golf? Nah. Never played it," Darren told him.

"That's funny, man," Bill replied with a laugh.

"What do you mean?" Darren said innocently.

"You don't play golf! Yeah, right! I think the people you've killed at the last two charity tournaments would disagree," Bill chuckled.

"Yeah," Darren said, smiling awkwardly. He couldn't imagine himself on the golf course and wondered if he would actually be able to play as his new self since he couldn't as his old one.

"Darren, are you going to get the steaks on the grill or let us starve?" Barbara called from the kitchen doorway.

Darren nodded toward her and reluctantly walked into the kitchen, unable to avoid Jennifer any longer. Their eyes met as he walked through the door and he quickly looked away. Was that recognition he saw? He was reaching for the steaks that had been marinating in the fridge when he heard Barbara excuse herself to Jennifer, now standing behind him.

"I'll be right back, Jennifer. I'm going to run down to the cellar and grab another bottle of wine," she said.

Darren turned around, container of steaks in hand, and found himself face-to-face with Jennifer once again. She looked as stricken as he felt, like a deer caught in headlights. Perhaps it was time to sort out what she did and didn't know. Rather than making an effort to get away, he decided to see what she knew.

"So, Jennifer. How long have you lived next door?" he asked, realizing that he didn't really know the answer to that either but just wanting to see how she responded.

"Seems like forever," she said. Her chest felt heavy as she skirted around the question. Was he fishing? Did he know?

"Yes, it does. You know, I don't think I've ever asked, but how long have you and Bill been married?" he asked, his heart racing.

"Five years," she replied. She did know the answer to that, thanks to an awkward moment when she had "forgotten" their anniversary recently.

"Still newlyweds, huh?" he asked.

"Yes. I suppose we are," she replied, feeling like he knew something, but afraid to ask.

Darren thought for a moment before asking yet another, more personal question. It could make things very strange if she didn't know anything. Then again, it could tell him and her that they both knew exactly what was going on. He thought maybe he shouldn't and excused himself to put the steaks on the grill. Moments later, he returned to the kitchen to rinse out the empty container they had been in and found that Barbara had still not returned. Jennifer seemed to have swilled down her drink rather quickly. Was she uncomfortable? Anxious?

"Would you like another drink?" he asked.

"Yes. That would be great," she replied a little too enthusiastically.

"Vodka, cranberry, and a dash of lime?" he asked knowingly, assuming that certain things about her remained the same if she was aware of what had happened as much as he was. The look in her eyes told him she knew and before she could answer, he added a phrase they used to laugh about. "Just like your mother used to make them when you were a child."

"You do know!" she exclaimed, her voice a mix of anguish and excitement.

"Yes. I do," he replied.

"Darren, what has happened to us? I didn't think you knew. If this is what you wanted, then I wanted you to be happy," she replied.

"That store Santa did this to us. I don't know how, but he did," he told her in a whisper, darting a quick glance out the window to make sure Bill was still watching the grill as it warmed up.

"Yes, of course. I wondered if that was possible, but I guess it has to be," she said, her face suddenly full of anger.

"I've missed you so much, Jennifer. I didn't really want any of this. I was just frustrated," he said, wanting to touch her but not doing so for fear of being caught.

"I've missed you too. I hate this new life. I don't know why I wished you away," she replied, her anger now fading into tearfulness.

"Listen, we can't talk here, but we need to sort this out. Just make the best of things tonight and tomorrow, meet me at the Blue Moon for lunch at noon. We'll talk this out and figure out how to fix it. There has to be a way to get things back to normal," he said in a hushed tone.

"Okay. I'm so glad you are still you," she said, her comments cut off there as Barbara's footsteps resounded up the basement stairs.

"Whew! I had a hard time choosing! You've put a lot of new stuff down there, darling," she said to Darren, kissing him on the cheek. He looked uncomfortable and pulled away, excusing himself out to the yard.

The rest of the evening seemed to drag out for both of them as they tried to play the parts they had been assigned and just get through it. At the end of the night, Bill and Jennifer returned to their home where she tossed and turned for hours after going to bed. She had almost accepted this new life, but she had never forgotten her love for Darren. Now, knowing he knew what was going on as well as she did, she would do whatever it took to get back to him.

***

The following day, Darren and Jennifer sat at the little out-of-the-way bistro in a neighboring town, holding hands across the table. It felt like the first time they had held hands way back when they had first met. Their voices were quiet so that they couldn't be overheard by anyone near them. It would all sound so crazy to anyone who might overhear.

"What do we do?" Jennifer asked, still feeling panicked at the thought that this was somehow beyond repair.

"I don't know. I lay awake all night trying to figure that out. I guess we just leave them and get back together. I mean, I feel bad about that. I don't know about Bill, but Barbara is a very good person and doesn't deserve to be hurt. She seems to genuinely love this new me, even though I've been distant to her. As much as I thought I'd want to be with a woman like that, she's not you. I'd rather be bickering with you about silly things than spending tranquil days by our pool with her," he said.

"I know what you mean. Bill is just as perfect as how I described him to that hack Santa, but I don't want him. All I think about every day is how much I miss our old life together. Things weren't perfect, far from it. You weren't perfect and neither was I, but I loved us. I wish we could have just found a way to meet each other halfway and not have done this to ourselves," she said glumly.

"I know how you feel, but what is done is done. All we can do is leave them and just pick up where we left off," he replied.

"Look on the bright side," Jennifer laughed. "At least you got out of Christmas with my mother."

"If we manage to get this straightened out, I'll go see your mother every weekend," Darren laughed. Jennifer joined him, both of them beaming at one another across the table.

"Okay, so what do we do?" Jennifer asked.

"Well, let's just go home, tell them that it isn't working out and that we're leaving. Pack your bags and meet me at the Stafford Hotel over on Finnegan Street there in town. We will stay there until we sort out getting a place to live, finances and all that. I think all of my money actually belongs to her except for what comes in the new business and probably the same with you and Bill, so we'll just have to manage until we get on our feet," he told her.

"That's okay. I'd rather spend a lifetime of poverty with you than one more day with that Stepford husband I've been assigned," Jennifer laughed.

"Okay. I don't think check-in is until two over there, so that gives us both time to pack and do whatever we need to do as far as making a hasty exit. I'll leave a key for you at the front desk," he replied.

"Perfect. I will be there," Jennifer replied happily. She was positively giddy to be getting her old husband back and now regretted that they hadn't known the truth sooner. They could have avoided all the time they had spent apart already. It was almost spring. They had lost months together.

Outside the bistro, they held each other in a tight embrace. Darren pulled her into a passionate kiss like they hadn't shared in years. It was if this had only brought them closer together and each was excited about rekindling their marriage, despite all the hurdles they would have to face.

"I love you so much, Jennifer," Darren breathed against her hair. She pulled away from him, looking up into his face as she stroked his cheek.

"I love you, too," Jennifer sighed.

They went their separate ways down the sidewalk toward their cars and made their way back to their homes feeling more hopeful than they had in months.

Chapter 5

Jennifer sat nervously at the breakfast table the next morning looking across the table at Bill as he sipped his coffee and smiled at her. He really was an incredible man. The perfect man, in fact. He was everything she had described to the store Santa and then some. She found herself wondering what would happen to him when she left. Would he get a new wife that he didn't realize he hadn't always been with? Would he cease to exist? Or would he be alone and devastated?

She felt sad at the thought of hurting such a good man. The problem was that she just didn't love him. As much as she had thought she wanted someone like him, it seemed that her heart still belonged to the impossible, imperfect husband she had known before this.

"Are you okay, honey?" he asked thoughtfully, sitting his cup down to study her face.

"Yes, I'm fine. I was just mentally running through the list of what I have to do today," she said. It was mostly the truth.

"Well, you seemed a little frazzled already. Don't overdo it," he told her, reaching across the table to pat her softly on the hand.

"I won't," she said with a smile.

"Is there anything I can do to help you?" he asked.

"No. I can handle it," she said, trying not to sound as guilty as she felt.

Seeing him off to work, she busied herself in getting ready to meet Darren as they had planned. Her sadness was quickly replaced by anticipation at the thought of getting back to her real husband and out of this way too perfect life that she couldn't stand.

***

Next door, Darren was preparing for what he told Barbara was an overnight trip out of town to visit with some investors in his business. She had no reason to think he was lying and accepted his explanation without question, even helping him pack some of his things before he shuffled her off so that he could pack those things that might tell her he planned on not coming back.

"Honey, don't forget your medication. You're never going to get rid of the remnants of the flu if you don't finish the cycle," she said.

"I think I will be fine. Thanks," he said. She was a thoughtful woman and he had been wondering why he was on antibiotics since he found the bottle, so that answered that question finally. He had wanted to ask before but knew it would be an odd question.

"You always say that. I think you must be the worst patient a doctor has ever seen," she laughed, running her hand down his back as she laid some perfectly folded boxer shorts by his suitcase for him to pack.

"Probably," he said, feeling quite bad about what he was doing to such a sweet woman. Still, she wasn't what he had wanted, after all. He had certainly thought she was when he had described her, but it seemed that the only person that really held any place in his heart was Jennifer.

"I'll go get breakfast started while you finish up here," she said. "I'm going to go shopping with some girls from my yoga class after we eat."

Darren nodded. He was way too jittery to eat breakfast and knew he would only feel worse sitting across the table from her, but it would get her out of here so that he could finish his packing. He could wait until she left to go shopping, but he was too anxious to put it off.

Once she was out of the room, he hurriedly added more clothes and shoes and sat on the suitcase to pack it down to a point that it wouldn't be so noticeable how full it had become. He felt the same sense of guilt as Jennifer had with Bill about hurting Barbara, but he knew that this wasn't where he belonged. No matter what he had said to that blasted supernatural Santa, this perfect life he had ordered didn't suit him at all. He wanted his old life back and yesterday couldn't be soon enough.

***

Jennifer ended up arriving at the hotel before Darren. They were nervous as they checked into their room at the hotel. It was an anxious anticipation like they hadn't felt since they first met. Part of it was due to being together again and part of it was just the not knowing what might happen.

"My wife and I have reservations," Darren told the clerk, handing him his license and credit card. He found that he couldn't make eye contact. It was if he was doing something wrong, but everything in his heart told him that it was right. After all, this was his real wife.

"Ah, very good. Let's just get you checked in and we will get you settled into your room," the clerk told him, punching some keys. Darren and Jennifer looked at each other a bit sheepishly, fidgeting with their bags while they waited.

"Okay, Mr. and Mrs. Johnson. Here are your room keys and there is a cart right there to your left that you can use to take your bags up the elevator to room 303. It will be on the right side of the hall about three doors down once you arrive on the third floor," he said politely.

Darren had noted that Jennifer was beaming as the clerk addressed her by her former married name and so he repeated it as they walked away, passing the cart by as they each only had one bag with them.

"Come on, Mrs. Johnson. We have some catching up to do," Darren told her as they made their way to their room. He smacked her playfully on the backside as she got ahead of him toward the elevator. She giggled a little and reached for his hand. To anyone passing by they seemed like an ordinary married couple, though what was happening with them was anything but ordinary. It was crazy, if anything.

They were barely in the door, dropping suitcases across the floor as they tumbled onto the bed. Darren's hands tangled in Jennifer's hair, kissing her in a way he hadn't for years. She clung to him as if he might disappear if she let go. There was certain urgency to their lovemaking, yet it was sweet, tender. They explored one another's bodies as if they'd never held one another before. Finally, things were back to the way they were supposed to be. Now, they could sort out everything else to get back to their old life as quickly as possible.

***

"I am so glad that we finally are back together," Jennifer said, rolling over to face Darren as the sun streamed through a nearby window. As her eyes focused on her surroundings she realized that she was no longer at the hotel and the man beside her was no longer Darren. Melancholy washed over her as her eyes fell upon the sleeping frame of Bill.

Bill's eyes opened, looking sleepy for a moment, but then opening wide. He sat up in bed and looked at her. He was obviously distraught and reached for her, pulling her close to him in a hug.

"Are you okay, Bill?" she asked.

"I was worried sick about you all night. When I woke up to find you lying next to me in bed as if nothing had happened, I was relieved that you were okay, but deeply hurt that you had just been so thoughtless and disappeared for hours on me like that. What happened?" he asked.

"I'm sorry, Bill. It couldn't be helped. I had a family emergency and just ran out without thinking. It was a crazy day," she said, trying not to look as shifty as she felt in lying to him.

"Oh, no. Is everything okay?" he asked, forgetting almost immediately, or so it seemed, that he had been upset with her.

"Yes. Things are fine, just a false alarm. I'm sorry I worried you so much," she told him. That much was true. He truly didn't deserve a lying, cheating wife, but what could she do in this unreal situation she and Darren had landed themselves in?

"It's fine. Don't worry your pretty head about it. Just try to take a moment to leave a note or call next time. I couldn't even reach your cell phone," he said, brushing a hair away from her face before kissing her on the forehead and making his way to the bathroom for his morning shower. It was apparent that he wasn't fine, but just like him to just accept and move on.

"I'm sorry," Jennifer said quietly to the closed door between them.

***

Next door, Darren rolled and put his arms around his sleeping partner. She stirred in his arms and cuddled against him.

"What are you doing back so soon?" she murmured sleepily. Darren's eyes shot open as he realized he was no longer at the hotel with Jennifer. He scurried out of bed to get dressed.

"I will tell you later, he managed, buying himself some time to come up with an excuse.

"I wasn't expecting you. I made plans with Betsy from spin class. I can cancel," she offered.

"No. Don't do that. I have a ton of work to do," he told her, already shuffling toward the door. Moments later he was in the study leaning against his desk with his head in his hands. How could this have failed? He barely registered Barbara telling him she was leaving.

Finally, the sound of her car starting jolted him from his trance and he hurried toward the back door, flinging it open and feeling some relief to see Jennifer pacing by the fence between their homes.

"What happened?" Jennifer asked.

"I don't know. I really felt that would work," Darren replied.

"What do we do now?" Jennifer asked.

"I have been thinking, perhaps we were too close. Going to a local place may not have been far enough," Bill replied.

"Where do you think we should go?" Jennifer asked.

"I don't know, maybe another town, maybe even another state," Darren replied.

"What about that little bed and breakfast we used to talk about going to but never got a chance to visit? It is just across the state line and will only take a few hours to drive there?" Jennifer suggested.

"It could work. What do we have to lose? Let's try to leave things a little more finished this time. We will leave them notes letting them know we left them and leave together. Just go pack your things and meet me out front in thirty minutes," Darren told her.

Jennifer nodded in agreement and ran back inside the house. Darren returned to his own and repacked the suitcase from yesterday, finding it was once again empty as if nothing had ever happened. He shook his head in disbelief and hurriedly prepared to leave, taking the time to write a note and leave it for Barbara on the kitchen counter. Once again, he felt a sense of guilt at what he was doing, but there was no other way.

***

The bed and breakfast seemed much further away than it actually was. Initially, they chattered nervously about what they were doing and expressed their hopefulness that it would work this time. However, as the trip continued, they fell into silence. Both were a nervous wreck by the time they reached their destination. Their anxiety quickly fell away as they found themselves alone again.

"It's going to work this time," Darren said softly as he held Jennifer close, kissing her neck.

"I hope so," she replied, letting passion replace the thoughts that clouded her mind.

Once again, they were are all over one another, making love most of the night, afraid of what would happen if they fell asleep. Sometime in the wee hours of the morning just before the daylight, they lost the battle and drifted quietly into sleep lying in one another's arms. As the sun streamed into the window of the room it cast shadows across their empty bed. Both Darren and Jennifer were downcast to find themselves once again waking in the beds of their ideal spouses.

***

"Bill, I am so sorry. The holidays have just been so stressful and I needed to get away. I should've sat down and talked to you, but I just didn't know what to say," Jennifer told her ideal spouse. Having failed twice, she feared she was stuck here with him and felt it best to try to make amends until she could figure this out.

"I just don't get it, Jennifer. This is the second time you have disappeared and your mom did not seem to know anything about the emergency last time," Bill replied.

"You called my mom to check up on me?" Jennifer asked.

"Yes and no. After I got your note I called her to check on you because I felt perhaps there was something I was missing. I thought we were happy, Jennifer, but things have been incredibly strange between us since Christmas," Bill replied.

"I know, Bill. I have just been in a strange place," Jennifer replied. It was as close to the truth as anything.

"And now? Are you all sorted out now?" Bill asked.

"Yes. I'm sorry. I don't know what I was thinking. I hope you can forgive me," Jennifer said in earnest.

"Don't worry about it. Everything will be fine. Just take the time to talk to me next time instead of running off. Okay?" Bill replied.

"I will. Thank you. I'm going to go lie down if you don't mind. We will talk later?" Jennifer said.

"Absolutely," Bill replied, flashing a warm smile.

Jennifer climbed the staircase to their bedroom and lay down, face first in the pillow. Her heavy sobs were muffled by the goose down as she cried herself to sleep. When she awoke, hours later, it was dark outside. She had no idea what Darren must be thinking and knew she should go to him, but she just couldn't muster the strength to leave the house and try to make contact. Instead, she got out of bed, showered and dressed to go down for dinner with Bill.

***

The following morning, Jennifer made her way down to the mailbox. She pulled from it the usual array of bills and advertisements before turning back toward the house. She was caught off guard as Darren darted out his front door and stopped in front of her.

"I missed you yesterday, but I thought maybe you needed to think," Darren told her.

"I did. I was so tired Darren. I just don't know how we can make this work. I'm absolutely miserable, but I think we are stuck this way," Jennifer said in a resigned tone of voice.

"Don't give up, Jennifer. We just made a mistake. That's all. We shouldn't have fallen asleep," Darren told her.

"How do you know that will even work?" Jennifer said, wearily.

"I don't. I can't see why it wouldn't though," Darren said.

"I can't keep going through this," Jennifer said solemnly.

"I know it's hard, Jennifer, but what choice do we have? Our only other alternative is to live out our lives with other people. I don't want that. Do you?" Darren asked.

Jennifer nodded, tears in her eyes. She knew that she couldn't spend her life with Bill. The problem was, she wasn't sure if she would be allowed to spend it with Darren either.

***

Darren and Jennifer came up with a new plan to return to the bed and breakfast one more time and ensure that they remained awake until the dawn. Later that night, they sneaked out after their spouses had gone to bed, met at the same bed and breakfast in the wee hours of the morning and sat up talking and drinking coffee, determined not to fall asleep. Of course, as time for dawn approached, they drifted off, unable to hold their eyes open any longer.

The following morning, they woke up to find that they were once again in the beds of their ideal spouses. Neither was any wiser that they had been gone. They each decided to just make the best of it. Perhaps they just had to go through the motions of getting a divorce in this world and remarrying one another, but would that even work if they were just going to wind up in their ideal spouse's bed every morning? After pondering every way thinkable, they came to separate conclusions that they had to find that store Santa. He had done this to them, so he must know how to undo it.

***

"We have to go to the mall," Jennifer said breathlessly. She had watched as Darren went out for a run that morning and had caught up with him once Bill was out of the house for the day. Now, facing him as he sipped the water he had holstered to his side, she watched a smile creep across his face.

"I know, but it doesn't open until ten," he told her, handing her the water.

Jennifer drank deeply, catching her breath as she smiled up at his handsome face. They both laughed and stood talking by the park where she had found him for a few moments.

"Okay. I'll go home and shower and meet you there when they open," she told him.

"Perfect. I'll go on ahead so you can make it home at your own pace and that no one sees us coming home together. And besides, we both know that you are a slowpoke and I don't want to embarrass you if we were to run home together," Darren said

"Funny guy now, huh? I might have to have a separate talk with this so-called Santa about some changes I'd like to make in you when I get you back," she joked.

"Nooooo. I think he has done enough! Who knows what will happen if we let him interfere again!" Darren scoffed. Laughing, he took off toward his house and Jennifer followed him, walking and daydreaming about how things used to be before all of this had happened. It seemed that the bad parts no longer mattered. All she could remember were the good times they had shared.

Chapter 6

"Excuse me? I'm looking for a Christmas Santa you had here in the mall," Darren told yet another person that worked there. He and Jennifer were already exhausted from asking everyone they could find. The information desk had sent them to security and security had told them to check with the department store that had hired the person to play Santa. Since they had met him wandering around the mall, neither knew which store had employed him and none of the ones they went to seemed inclined to assist them in finding out

"Dude, it's March! I'm pretty sure he's back at the North Pole by now," a young hipster told them as he put away some hangers behind the customer service desk of the last one they went to. Both of their shoulders fell as they began to realize they might never find him.

"Thanks a lot, pal," Darren said sarcastically as they turned to leave.

"I'm starving. Let's at least grab a bite to eat before we go," Jennifer said.

"What if someone sees us and will tell Barbara or Bill?" Darren asked, looking around.

"If they haven't seen us by now, they aren't going to," Jennifer replied. Her face revealed how tired she had become and Darren acquiesced, walking with her to the food court.

"I just don't get how he could have disappeared," Darren said glumly.

"I don't get how he could have magically given us new lives," Jennifer replied.

"True, but here we are, aren't we?" Darren replied as they approached the large open area filled with tables and surrounded by a half moon of assorted fast food restaurants.

They split up to buy food at separate places, something they had always done as a couple. Darren liked the carb loaded slices of pizza at the Italian place and Jennifer preferred the fresh veggie rolled sandwiches made by the Greek restaurant a little farther down. It was one of the few differences they had dealt with in their previous life that had an easy solution. They ate and then headed back through the main portion of the mall toward the parking garage so they could head home.

"Darren, wait!" Jennifer suddenly said excitedly. "That girl. I recognize her. She was one of the elves that was hanging around near that Santa."

"Are you sure? It's been a while and she doesn't look familiar to me," he replied, looking at the girl to whom Jennifer was pointing through a shop window.

"It's her. She has a birthmark on her neck. See? Right there on the back of it. I noticed it when she turned around, right before he started talking to me," Jennifer insisted.

"Well, can't hurt. Let's go talk to her," Darren replied, not feeling terribly encouraged after all the dead ends of the day. They walked into the shop and waited for the girl to finish with the customer she was with.

"Excuse me, but weren't you working as an elf here during the holidays?" Jennifer asked her.

"Oh, yeah. Ugh. I needed the extra cash and they suckered me into that," she said, looking a little embarrassed by it.

"Do you know the guy that was in the Santa suit? He wasn't one of the one ones in the department stores. This one was wandering around by himself greeting people and he was near you at one point. I thought you might have been working with him," Jennifer told her.

"Oh, yeah. I know him. He's the one that got me the gig," she replied. "Why do you want to know?"

"It's a really long story, but we need to get in touch with him. Would you happen to have a phone number for him?" Darren asked.

"Phone? No. He hates phones. Won't use one. If you want to talk to him, you pretty much just have to catch him at home," she said with a laugh.

"You have his address then?" Jennifer asked.

The girl eyed them both suspiciously, looking from one to the other for a few moments before speaking again. It was obvious from her tone that she had become unsure of their intentions.

"You got some kind of beef with him? I don't want to be involved in anything like that," she said.

"No, absolutely not. We just need to talk to him, nothing more," Darren told her, smiling in a way that he hoped was calming and friendly.

"I tell you what. You need something. I need something. I'm behind on my sales quota this week. If you buy like $500 worth of merchandise, I will give you his home address."

Jennifer could see Darren stiffen, angry at being taken advantage of, but this was not the time for any of that. She quickly jumped in.

"Fine. Give us a few minutes," she said, pulling him aside to speak in private.

"Jennifer, she's blackmailing us!" Darren said.

"Do you want the address or not?" Jennifer asked, her voice a whisper. "Throw some money at the problem and let's get on with it, Darren."

Twenty minutes later, the two of them walked out of the little home décor shop with bags full of items that they neither wanted nor needed. Of more value to them was the address scrawled on the back of their receipt. Forgetting all about anyone seeing them, they dumped their shopping contents in the trunk of Darren's car and jumped in, heading directly to the address they had been given. It only took them about ten minutes to arrive, both remaining silent as they made their way out of the mall parking lot and into a subdivision down the highway that traveled past the main entrance. Both were nervous and tense as they waited for the door to be answered.

"Hello. Can I help you?" the man said as he opened the door. Both Jennifer and Darren were speechless for a moment. It was him!

"Yes. We need to talk to you about the little number you pulled on us at the mall this past Christmas," Darren said, his anger suddenly coming through loud and clear.

"Whoa, man. What are you talking about?" the guy said, carefully holding onto the door in case he needed to shut and lock it.

"Don't play stupid with me, man," Darren replied in a mocking tone. "You asked us what our Christmas wish was and when we each told you, you somehow made it come true. Our lives are completely screwed up because of you!"

"What? That's crazy. If I could grant wishes, do you think I'd be living in a crappy little rancher in this neighborhood?" the guy told him.

"All I know is that you did it. I don't know how. I don't know why, but I know you did it," Darren told him. They guy looked at him, wide eyed, and then turned his gaze toward Jennifer.

"You need to calm your old man here down. I don't know what he is on, but he is talking some serious nonsense. What he needs is a good shrink. As a matter of fact, I have a business card in my pocket that my probation officer gave me this morning. I think you need it more than I do," the guy laughed. He fished a card out of his pocket and tossed it toward Darren, slamming the door. The locks sounded loudly as they barred entry. Darren began beating on it as Jennifer reached down to pick up the card.

"Darren, stop. He's not going to answer and you'll end up getting arrested," she said.

Darren's face was red with anger as he turned back toward her, noting the card in her hand. He seemed to calm a bit as he looked it over.

"This might be the answer. I don't know why we have to jump through his little hoops, but I think we have to visit this guy to fix things," he said. Jennifer nodded in agreement.

Believing that it was what they must do for this "Santa" to fix what he did to them, they called the number on the card on their way back to Jennifer's car and made an appointment with Dr. Goodman.

Chapter 7

"Okay, Mr. and Mrs. Johnson, that is quite a story you have to tell," the psychologist told them a few days later in his office.

"It's not a story," Darren said in an agitated tone. Jennifer quietly slid her hand atop his to soothe him and he glanced at her, calming down as she smiled softly.

"Dr. Goodman, we know that what we are telling you sounds like a fantastic story we've made up, but it is absolutely true and we believe that you know it is. There should be a reason why we were sent here, so we just need to know what to do to fix this," Jennifer told him.

"Well, let's talk a bit about your relationship with one another and see what our best options are," he offered. "Let's start with how you met one another. Darren, would you like to go first?'

"Sure, okay. Well, it was our junior year of college. We had a class together and really hit it off. I remember being struck by her right away. She was smiling and it just lit up her whole face. I was surprised one night when one of my friends was having a party and Jennifer was there. I could hear her laughing and it seemed to beckon me from all the way across the room, but it still took me almost an hour to get up the courage to talk to her outside of class," he laughed. He looked pensive as he spoke, remembering the moment when everything had taken a turn from friendship to dating.

"I didn't know that. You seemed so sure of yourself when you came over," Jennifer said to him.

"Jon Ensley gave me a shot of tequila to calm myself and a stick of gum to cover it up," he laughed.

"I can't believe you kept that to yourself for so long," Jennifer laughed.

"Me either," Darren said, laughing with her. 'I thought I'd told you absolutely everything there was to know by now."

"So, the two of you don't have a problem sharing then?" the doctor interjected.

"No, I don't think we've ever really had any secrets from one another. Dishonesty has never been an issue," Jennifer told him.

"Then, what was an issue?" Dr. Goodman asked.

The couple looked at one another, realizing that nothing they would say next mattered. Everything that had been a problem between them suddenly seemed so trivial. It was obvious that they had let the small things in life get the better of them.

"Darren complained that I stopped taking care of myself, that I didn't dress up for him," Jennifer finally said.

"Is that true?" the doctor asked.

"Well, yes. I worked long hours as a realtor sometimes and so, had appearances to keep up. Wearing suits and heels all day can get uncomfortable. It just felt better when I was at home or on my off days to wear something that felt better on me," Jennifer said.

"What do you think about what Jennifer just said, Darren?" the doctor said, turning toward him.

"I guess I hadn't considered it, really. Usually, if I commented on it, she just acted hurt or angry and it turned into a huge thing," Darren said, looking a little ashamed to not have considered her side.

"And now that you know that side of things?" the doctor pushed.

"Well, I feel bad that I hadn't realized it. I would still have liked for her to take some time to look good just for us every once in a while but understand a bit better why she didn't do it every day. I just took it personally, like she didn't care about me and I wasn't worth the effort," Darren admitted.

"Jennifer, what do you think about that?" the doctor asked.

"I didn't think about it making him feel I didn't care about him. It had nothing to do with him in my view. I can understand why he felt that way," she said.

The couple's eyes met and they smiled, touching hands on the sofa between them. The doctor didn't say anything right away, giving them a bit of time to have this moment before continuing. After their hour was up, they left hand in hand, having learned a lot more about one another than they had ever considered. Perhaps it had been good for them to have someone sit down with them. Even though they both knew they missed one another and wanted to be together again, all of the old problems might have resurfaced if not dealt with once and for all.

Several more sessions passed during which they remained with their ideal spouses. There was no point in trying to be together if they were only going to wake up in the wrong bed every morning anyway. So, they carried on like a pair of secret lovers, spending time together in out of the way places where they wouldn't be seen together. Their new spouses were both still being very understanding about the vague excuses and explanations for a lack of intimacy and time away from home they were being given. It was obvious that it would always be that way with them, as they were very much the people Jennifer and Darren had requested them to be.

Still, they were reaching a point of frustration with the doctor, who still had provided them no solutions to their problem.

***

"So, Jennifer and Darren, it seems that we have worked through quite a few of the issues you had interfering with a happy marriage. Would you agree?" Dr. Goodman asked.

"Yes, but the biggest problem remains," Darren replied.

"Yes. You have said that no matter what you do, you return to these ideal spouses that you believe you were assigned by a magical Santa of some sort," the doctor replied.

"We *were* given new spouses by him. Spouses somehow designed to fit the bill for what we told him we wanted," Jennifer said.

"I'm afraid that there is really nothing I can do to change that," the doctor told them.

"What!?" Darren shrieked. He was suddenly on his feet, angry.

"Please sit down, Mr. Johnson. As I was saying, I can't change that. I am a psychologist, not a supernatural witch doctor of some sort. The best I can offer the two of you is a procedure that I can perform removing your memories of one another," he said.

"Remove our memories? No way!" Jennifer told him.

"Not all of your memories. Just the ones that involve you and Mr. Johnson. You have to consider that it might be better to just not remember your past lives than it is to be stuck in one where you are miserable about being apart," he told them.

"So, you believe us then?" Darren asked.

"I believe that you believe it and that is enough to make this type of procedure something worth considering," Dr. Goodman replied, seeming quite earnest. "Just go home, think it over for a few days and give me a call. I can set you up an appointment for early next week. It's done right here in the office using a combination of electrical stimulations and hypnotic suggestion. You will walk out with no memory of one another and can get on with your lives peacefully."

Darren and Jennifer both looked at the floor. It wasn't what they had wanted to hear, not even close. After leaving the doctor's office, they sat in Jennifer's car and discussed it for a bit before agreeing it wasn't something they could make up their minds about today. They parted with a kiss and a hug, returning separately to their homes as they usually did

Chapter 8

After some careful consideration on both their parts, Darren and Jennifer agreed that having their memories erased was the only way to escape the misery they feel without one another. They spent their final days of knowing one another suffering through seeing one another across the fence and at community events.

"Jennifer, I need to talk to you for a minute," Darren whispered. She had not heard him approach as she stood looking at vegetables on display at the local farmers market.

"Did you follow me here? Let's not make this worse," Jennifer said in a hushed tone.

"I don't know how it can be any worse. Tomorrow will take away everything we have ever known about one another. Before that happens, I'd like to spend at least one more night together. It may be all we have left," Darren told her, looking around to be sure no one was seeing him.

"That sounds nice," Jennifer replied.

"Meet me at the hotel, room 303, tonight at six," Darren told her, slipping away before she could even answer.

***

"I will go on this brief business trip and will be back in the morning, most likely before you are even up," Darren told Barbara. At least that much was a truth of which they could both be certain. No matter where he went, he would definitely be in her bed again come morning.

"Okay, honey. I will miss you," she told him brightly.

"I know," he replied, unable to even bring himself to tell her he would miss her too. Though she was a lovely person, she might as well be a stranger to him. He could only hope that, after this procedure, he would feel differently if he were to be doomed to spend his life with her.

Next door, Jennifer was having a similar discussion with Bill, telling him that her mother didn't feel well and she was going to spend the night with her. He accepted it without question and gave her a peck on the cheek as she left the house, standing in the doorway waving to her as she left. Once she cleared the door, she phoned her mother.

"Mom, I told Bill I was coming over there for the night. If he happens to call, I need to make sure he thinks I'm there," Jennifer told her.

"You want me to lie to Bill?" her mother replied.

"Yes. I know you don't like doing that, but this is important," Jennifer replied.

"Are you okay, honey?" her mother asked.

"I'm fine. I just have something I need to do. I need for you to not ask questions," Jennifer told her.

"Well, I just hope you know what you are doing," her mom replied.

"Thanks, Mom. I will talk to you soon," Jennifer said before ending the call.

***

Jennifer and Darren returned to the hotel where they had originally attempted to leave this new life behind and be together again. There was a certain air of sadness about both of them as they checked into their room, but they tried not to let it cloud their final hours of knowing one another.

Their bodies moved slowly against one another as they made love for the last time, knowing that they would never be together in this way again after tonight. Lying in the glow of their lovemaking, Darren's hands tangled in Jennifer's hair as he kissed her softly. She returned his kiss wholeheartedly as tears fell down her face.

"Don't cry, Jennifer," he said. "I hate to see tears on your face."

"I'm sorry. I was trying not to, but I just am going to miss you so much," she said.

"You won't miss me. All of this will be gone. Tonight and every night before it. No more pain of not being together. I'm sorry I did this to us," he said.

"It wasn't just you. We both did it," she said, choking back more tears.

"Yes, but I drove you to it with all my criticism and complaining. If I had been a better husband, you wouldn't have wanted a new one. If I had been a better provider, you wouldn't have had to work so hard all the time. I did everything wrong and then I blamed you for it. Even worse, I asked for someone to replace you. Now, all I can think about is how to get back everything we lost together," he told her.

"No. It wasn't all your fault. I never gave you a chance to make a better life for us. All those dreams you had about starting your own publishing house . . . I squashed them. I was so afraid that we would lose everything that I never stopped to realize how brilliant you are and that you could make it work. Look at you now, you are making it work. The publishing business you've been building in your new life is really taking off and in only a few months. Perhaps you are better off with her," Jennifer said, her voice almost a whisper.

"Don't say that, Jennifer. You were just trying to protect us. I love you and I always will, even if I don't remember how much I do," Darren told her, holding her to his chest tightly.

"I love you, too," Jennifer said, sobbing softly against his chest.

They fell asleep in one another's arms and when they awoke the next morning, each was lying next to their ideal spouse once again. The morning weighed heavily on their minds as they went about their usual routines and tried to prepare themselves for their visit to the doctor's office in a few hours.

Chapter 9

Sitting anxiously in the psychologist's office, Darren and Jennifer waited to be taken back for their procedures. They sat holding hands as Jennifer leaned her head against his arm, an incredible melancholy possessing each of them.

"Mr. and Mrs. Johnson?" Dr. Goodman's assistant called out to them. It hurt Jennifer to know that, after today, that salutation would only be used when addressing Darren and his new spouse.

"I guess this is it then. Let me look at you one last time. I love you so much, Jennifer," Darren told her as he stroked his finger down the side of her face.

"Yes, I suppose it is. Thank you for everything we've shared. I may not remember it soon, but I think that somewhere down deep, I will always know that I once had a great love that I had to give up," Jennifer told him, fighting back yet more tears.

"I don't want you to cry anymore, Jennifer. This will take the pain away," Darren told her, leaning in for one last kiss. It lingered until the assistant called them once again, causing them to pull away and finally let go of one another's hand.

***

"Okay, Mr. Johnson. Let's get you all set up for the procedure and then we will begin. Are you ready?" Dr. Goodman asked.

"Yes, Dr. Goodman," Darren replied. His heart felt as if it might beat out of his chest as the doctor busied himself on a nearby tray, preparing the leads to the equipment that would both monitor and stimulate him while the procedure was taking place. When the doctor approached him with one of the pads to put into place, Darren suddenly bolted forward.

"No. I can't. I can't give up what I have left of her," Darren said.

"Darren, this is certainly up to you, but you won't be able to find peace without this, I'm afraid. It may even be worse for you when Jennifer has no memory of what you've shared," Dr. Goodman counseled him.

"I don't care, Dr. Goodman. I want to keep my memories. If all I can have is being her neighbor and just seeing her face from time to time, then that is what I will live with. Just don't tell her I opted out. Let her have the procedure done and enjoy her peace of mind. I want that for her," Darren told him.

"I must urge you to reconsider, Darren," the doctor told him. "I fear this could have consequences to your mental health."

"My mind is made up. I won't lose what little I have left," Darren insisted.

"Okay, Mr. Johnson. That being the case, you are free to go. I wish you all the best and, of course, I will be here if you change your mind or simply need counseling in the future. In fact, I recommend that you continue with separate sessions for at least a while," Dr. Goodman told him.

"Thanks. I'll let you know," Darren told him. He left the office hurriedly, knowing how painful it was going to be next time he saw Jennifer and there was no flicker in her eyes of the life they had shared.

Inside, Dr. Goodman moved to the small procedure room on the opposite side of his office and entered, smiling broadly at Jennifer.

"Are you ready, Jennifer?" he asked.

"Listen, Dr. Goodman. I have been thinking about all of this and I've decided that I don't want to have the procedure done. I only came here because I don't want Darren to know that I still have my memories. I want for him to be happy with his new life but I don't want to lose everything we have shared together over the years. He is just too important to me," she told him.

"Jennifer, you are miserable now. Do you not think it will be harder living next to him when he is embracing his new life with someone else? He won't remember you at all after his procedure is complete," Dr. Goodman told her, knowing that he couldn't reveal the truth.

"I understand. I know it won't be easy, but I rather be able to see his face every day and know he is happy than to spend the rest of my life oblivious to what we used to have together," she told him.

Dr. Goodman sighed and shrugged his shoulders. "Okay, Jennifer. If that is the case and you are sure, then we are done here. If you change your mind or need to come back in to just talk through things, just make an appointment. In fact, I recommend it. I will be more than happy to see you," he told her.

"I won't need the procedure or the therapy, Dr. Goodman, but thank you for everything," she told him, grabbing her purse and heading for the door. She noted that Darren's car was no longer in the parking lot, but assumed he had already finished his treatment. Starting her car, she returned home.

Chapter 10

"Are you feeling okay, Jennifer?" Bill asked as he stood in the doorway to their bedroom, watching her put on her makeup.

"Yes, I'm fine. I am almost ready," she told him, slipping her earrings on and looking at herself in the mirror.

"You look absolutely stunning," Bill told her.

"Thank you. You look quite handsome in your suit, as well," she replied. She had realized that if she were going to move on with her life without Darren, she would have to embrace the new life with Bill, as well. Perhaps in time, she would grow to care for him, but she found it hard to believe that she could ever be truly in love with anyone other than Darren.

"I am just glad they didn't make me wear a monkey suit. Only the Palatkas would have a semi-formal party for St. Patrick's Day!" he laughed. Jennifer laughed with him and stood, admiring herself in the full length mirror standing nearby as he headed back downstairs to wait. She thought of Darren and how he would have loved to see her in something like this, a shimmering black cocktail dress with just a hint of green for the occasion.

The thought brought with it more of the sadness she had been feeling and she let it wash over her for a few moments before taking a deep breath and joining Bill for the party. She felt like being anywhere but headed to a festive event, but this was her life now. This is where she had painted herself into a permanent corner.

After a couple of hours at the party, she just could no longer fake a smile and felt as if she might scream soon. Knowing that Darren was now lost to her and there was nothing she could do to change it made her physically ill. Making excuses to their hosts, she told Bill she needed to go home.

"I'm sorry. Perhaps it was something you ate. Let me say a quick goodbye and I'll drive you," he told her.

"No. You just stay here and enjoy the party. I know you have a lot of contacts you were hoping to make tonight and I'm fine, really. It's probably just a bug or something. I'll catch a cab and just see you when you get in," she told him.

"Are you sure? I don't want to leave you all alone if you are sick," he said.

"I'm positive. Have fun. I will see you at home," she said. He leaned forward and kissed her cheek as she made her way out of the large hall their friends the Palatkas had rented for their event. Whistling for a cab, she climbed into the back and leaned against the cool leather of the seat. She felt mentally exhausted by the time the cab pulled into her own driveway. Her breath caught in her throat as she saw the light going out in Darren's bedroom window next door and tears fell down her face as she thought about someone else holding him, loving him.

A half hour later, she was changed into her nightgown and climbing into the large empty bed she would now share with Bill. She felt weary to the bone and fell asleep almost as soon as her head hit the large, overstuffed pillows.

***

"I can't wait to get to the Harrisons! They always have the best barbecues! I think we will have a lot of fun today," Barbara had chirped as she practically glided into the kitchen where Darren had decided it was time for a cold beer. You could always see her former model training in the way she walked and carried herself. Any man would be lucky to have her as a wife. Yet, here he was, only wanting Jennifer back. The decision earlier today not to have his memories erased had been a tough one.

With time, perhaps it would be easier to let her go. He hadn't seen her since he had returned from the doctor. He had purposely avoided it, in fact. Seeing the lack of recognition in her eyes might just be the most painful thing of all. Now, that part of her was gone, the part of her that loved him was lost, along with all of the memories that had been a part of their lives.

"I'll let you drive. I am going to finish my beer and then we will go," he told Barbara. She looked at him quizzically and then walked over.

"Sure, honey. Are you okay? It seems as if something is bothering you," she told him.

"I'm fine. Sorry. Just had a tough day," he told her. That had to be the understatement of the year. No doubt about it.

As they made their way out the front door to the car, he noted that Jennifer and Bill's car was already gone. No doubt they were off to a party of their own, Jennifer now oblivious to his existence. He felt as if a gray cloud hung over him, shadowing him as he meandered unexcitedly toward their car and got into the passenger's side.

Hours later, after far too many beers and more food than any human should consume, Darren just couldn't take it anymore. All these happy people around him were having the time of their life and he smiled and nodded as if he were too, but inside, he felt like he was dying. Barbara was still flitting around from person to person, ever the social butterfly. He walked over and pulled her to one side, out of earshot of the others.

"Barb, I am not feeling all that well. I'm going to go back to the house and lie down," he told her.

"Oh, honey. I'm sorry. I'll take you right now," she said.

"No. You look like you are having a lot of fun and I know how much you love these barbecues. I'll just walk. It isn't that far and the night air will do me some good," he told her.

"I don't know, Darren. You've had a few beers. Let me drive you," she insisted.

"I'm fine. I promise. I will see you later at home," he told her.

"Okay then, but call me when you get there so that I know you are okay," she told him as he walked away. He nodded slowly in acknowledgement and walked the three-quarters of a mile back to their house. He had hoped the quiet streets and a nice breeze would clear his head, but it had only given him more time to think about Jennifer.

Even as he entered the house and sent Barbara a text saying he was home, he felt the wetness on his face. He hadn't cried in a very long time, but here he was. After climbing the stairs, he slipped into his pajamas and got into bed, eager to bury his face beneath the covers and forget the world for a while.

***

Darren awoke the next morning to find it looking dreary outside the bedroom window. Was that snow? It wasn't unheard of, but very unusual for it to snow in March. As his eyes adjusted to his surroundings, he turned toward the pillow beside him and his heart began to beat wildly.

"Jennifer! Wake up. We're back. We're back!" he practically sang to her.

Jennifer sat bolt upright in bed and looked around incredulously. They were back in their old bedroom and their bed. Was it really over?

"Are we really here? In our house? Together?" she asked, almost afraid to get her hopes up.

"Yes! I think we are," Darren said, pulling her to him and kissing her as if she were the last woman on the planet. After a while, they pulled away from one another, almost afraid to let go.

"I love you, Darren. I'm so happy we are home again!" she told him.

"I love you, too, Jennifer. I wonder what did it? How did we finally get back?" he pondered.

"I don't know, but I am never going to be stupid enough to take you for granted again," she told him.

"We are going to promise each other right now that we will never take each other for granted again and that we will talk more about what is bothering us instead of just lashing out," Darren told her.

"I completely agree," Jennifer told him. "Now that we are back to where we belong, there is nothing that we can't face together."

"Let's get some breakfast. I'm suddenly starving!" Darren told her.

"Me too. I guess I didn't eat much last night," she told him, jumping out of bed and heading to the closet. It was wonderful to see all of her old things again and she quickly chose a pair of casual slacks and a short-sleeved shirt.

"I seriously believe you might want to rethink that," Darren laughed, pointing toward the window.

"Snow? It's March, for heaven's sake!" she said, slipping into the pants, but exchanging the shirt for a warm red sweater. It was one of her favorites. Darren had given it to her for a birthday present in the winter. She slipped on a pair of leather boots and took the time to fix her hair and makeup while he quickly dressed and headed downstairs. The smell of bacon wafted up through the air. When she got to the kitchen, he was setting out plates on the table for them to enjoy a nice hot breakfast together.

"I thought we were going out to breakfast?" she teased.

"We are going out, but not to breakfast. I think today we should just get out and do something fun. We can do anything you would like," he told her.

"Let's go to the park and just go for a walk in the cool air. Hopefully, it is not too brisk out there," she said.

"We'll give it a shot," he replied.

After they ate, they gathered their coats and headed to the front door. A blast of cold air hit them in the face as they stepped out onto the front porch and looked around at the falling snow.

"No way can we go for a walk in this," Darren said.

"You've got that right!" Jennifer laughed. "How can it be so cold in the spring?

"Look how deep it is getting! I've never seen it snow this much during this time of year," Darren told her.

"Me either," she said, picking up a handful and rolling it into a ball which she threw at him, hitting him squarely in the chest.

"Oh, it's like that, huh?" he laughed, stepping into the front yard to make his own snowball. Jennifer ran out with him, dropping into the snow to make a snow angel just as his return throw went sailing over her head. They were like two kids with a snow day off from school.

"Looks like you folks are having, fun! Merry Christmas!" a voice called out to them from nearby.

"Christmas? It's spring!" Darren replied back, turning to see who the voice belonged to.

"Afraid not, my friend. It's Christmas Day!" the man said, whistling as he walked past them in a long winter coat. As he looked up toward them, they each recognized him as the Christmas Santa and headed toward him, but he disappeared quickly into the snow as it began to fall even heavier, sending them scurrying back inside.

"Christmas Day? It's like it never happened. We are right back where we left off," Jennifer said incredulously.

"We sure are. I guess we'll head over to your mom's house then," Darren said with a smile.

"Sure. When the snow lets up, but first, I think we should snuggle back up in bed. It's really cold out there," Jennifer purred.

"I think I like that idea," Darren replied, grabbing her hand and pulling her to the bedroom.

***

As the years passed, Jennifer and Darren never forgot what had happened to them. Their lives were changed forever by an event they couldn't share with anyone although it had brought them closer together than ever. The years unfolded to bring them not only success in the eventual opening of Darren's publishing house, but a beautiful daughter they named Destiny. It was she that one Christmas brought home a brightly colored tin to present to her parents after an outing with her grandmother.

"Open it, open it!" she exclaimed, handing it to Jennifer.

Jennifer took it, smiling at Darren until she noticed he wasn't smiling back. His eyes were riveted on the tin in her hands, a puzzled look on his face. Jennifer followed his gaze and gasped involuntarily, almost dropping it.

"What's wrong? Don't you like it? You haven't even seen what's inside," Destiny said, sounding disappointed.

"Oh, honey. Of course we do," Jennifer replied.

She slowly removed the top to reveal homemade peppermint bark with a small card on top. It displayed a rosy-cheeked Santa on the front. On the inside it read, *"May all your Christmas wishes bring you a lifetime of joy."*

Jennifer and Darren exchanged glances and looked back at their smiling daughter. She was obviously pleased with herself.

"It's wonderful," Darren said. "Where did you get such a lovely gift?"

"Grandma helped me make the bark," Destiny replied. "I got the tin and the card from one of those Santas down at the mall. He even let me make a Christmas wish."

Both Jennifer and Darren looked at one another again with raised eyebrows of concern. After a moment, during which they felt very ill at ease, Darren managed to ask the question on each of their minds.

"What did you wish for?" Darren asked.

"Santa said I couldn't tell or it would not come true," Destiny replied.

The rest of the day was filled with a bit of unease as Darren and Jennifer contemplated what their daughter might have asked for. The following morning, they each awoke reaching for one another to make sure they were still together. Though it was not likely that Destiny would have asked for anything that might separate them, it was still a relief to find themselves in the same bed in their own house.

Just as they were rising to head downstairs Destiny came through their bedroom door. She was all smiles as she held up a pudgy brown puppy for them to see.

"Look!" she squealed. "I got a puppy just like I wished for! It was under the Christmas tree."

Both Jennifer and Darren breathed a sigh of relief and followed their daughter downstairs as her new puppy clambered down the steps behind her. Neither had bought her a puppy, but that was not a surprise. As they stood in the middle of the living room, Jennifer's eyes fell on the table where the Christmas tin filled with peppermint bark still lay. The image pictured on top of the tin once again caught her eye as a familiar Santa stood smiling with a happy couple that she recognized as Bill and Barbara.

What to read next?

If you liked this book, you will also like *The Weekend Girlfriend*. Another interesting book is *Two Reasons to Be Single*.

The Weekend Girlfriend

Jessica has worked hard to be the paralegal that hotshot, sexy attorney Kyle needs. Unfortunately he doesn't see her as just his paralegal but also his own personal assistant. When he blames her for a mix-up in his personal life, Jessica sees no other option but to quit, thinking that her time with him is over. Much to her surprise, Kyle makes a proposition to her that she never thought she would hear coming from his lips. He needs a temporary girlfriend for his sister's wedding and he wants her to be that person. Jessica accepts the challenge and finds herself thrown into his world, learning things about him she never knew. The more time she spends with him outside of work, the more she is drawn to Kyle. As the wedding draws near, she finds herself fighting off some strong feelings for the man. When the wedding weekend is over, will Jessica be able to walk away from Kyle with her heart intact?

Two Reasons to Be Single

Olivia Parker has a job doing what she loves, a wonderful family and plenty of friends, but no luck in the love department. Tired of worrying about it, she decides to swear off love completely and focus on all the good things in her life. Just as she makes her firm resolution, Jake Harper arrives in town and knocks her plans into a tailspin. As the excited single ladies of Morning Glory surround the extremely attractive newcomer, Olivia steers clear of the "casserole brigade," as she calls the women, and tries to keep her distance from Jake. Instead, a variety of situations throw them together and they get to know each other better. They both have reasons for not wanting to get involved in a relationship, but the chemistry between them ignites, even as they desperately attempt to keep it at bay. As things heat up between Olivia and Jake, there is an aura of mystery about him that leaves Olivia certain that he is hiding something. When Jake disappears for a few days without telling Olivia that he is going out of town, she hates the way it makes her feel, and it reminds her of why she was giving up on dating in the first place. As Olivia's feelings for Jake grow, so does the need to find out what exactly brought him to Morning Glory and what he's been hiding.

About Emily Walters

Emily Walters lives in California with her beloved husband, three daughters, and two dogs. She began writing after high school, but it took her ten long years of writing for newspapers and magazines until she realized that fiction is her real passion. Emily likes to create a mental movie in her reader's mind about charismatic characters, their passionate relationships and interesting adventures. When she isn't writing romantic stories, she can be found reading a fiction book, jogging, or traveling with her family. She loves Starbucks, Matt Damon and Argentinian tango.

One Last Thing...

If you believe that *The Christmas Gift* is worth sharing, would you spend a minute to let your friends know about it?

If this book lets them have a great time, they will be enormously grateful to you – as will I.

Emily

www.EmilyWaltersBooks.com

Made in the USA
Columbia, SC
02 November 2020